I0761872

Deep in Darkness

By George Spain

Ideas into Books: Westview®
Kingston Springs, Tennessee

Ideas into Books®
W E S T V I E W
P.O. Box 605
Kingston Springs, TN 37082
www.publishedbywestview.com

This book is a work of fiction. Names, characters, places and incidents either are products of the author's imagination or are used fictitiously. Any resemblance to actual events or locales or persons, living or dead, is entirely coincidental.

ISBN 978-1-62880-191-0

First edition, October 2019

Printed in the United States of America on acid free paper.

From ghoulies and ghosties
And long-legged beasties
And things that go bump in the night,
Good Lord, deliver us.

Scottish prayer

TABLE OF CONTENTS

Introduction 1
The Black Boar 3
Codicil to My Will 5
The Twin 29
Blood for Blood 33
Halloween 1946 45
God's Punishment 51
The Whippoorwill Calls at Night 59
The Spirit 67
Lafe 75
Runes 85
Beneath the Stairs 89
Wolf Skin 105
Come Sit With Me 117

INTRODUCTION

Life is so full of strangeness and oddities it makes you wonder at times, "What'n the devil is going on?" Beyond strange, there are some things that even the Bible, Freud, Darwin, astrophysics, and plain old thinking don't explain well enough to suit me – things that are just downright scary.

The stories you are about to read come from two families: mine and my wife's and from long hours of research done in the Tennessee State Archives. They are as true as I can make them.

THE BLACK BOAR

Deep in darkness   deeper than shadows

    quiet

        listening

Hearing dreams curve   relax

Then catch tight at last

On tusks   curving   always curving

    inward

        tighter

Rooting time away   his small eyes burn

Remembering with fire

Almost the laurel thicket has light forever

    a burning bush

        almost

But only blackness and dumbness

Grunting   slowly   grunting

Something that has no meaning

    over

        and over

Wallowing deeper into the cool mountain

Of his birth   floating on dreams

His ancient reflection flowing away in darkness

    quiet

        listening

Hearing horns blowing away the forest

    black

        bristling.

CODICIL TO MY WILL

of

May *1, 1861*

To Benjamin Pearson Magruder, my beloved son "Ben", I am attaching this codicil to my will so you will understand that you are not to blame for any of the horrors that have come to our family. What I have done is for one purpose only—to protect you. I love you more than life itself. Know this from me: There is no demon in you; there is only goodness. May God bless you and keep you.

Be it known to all, what I write here of our family is true. I swear it on my mother's Bible, which lies before me, so help me God!

******

On June 10, 1865, in Maury County Tennessee, one month after the war ended, Ben discovered my father's body in the boxwood garden behind Father's house. The force of the pistol ball to his head had knocked him backward against the iron bench beneath an arbor of pink roses. The arbor stands at the far end of a long brick walkway sided by two rows of dark green boxwoods. Father's derringer lay on the ground beside him. Though he left no note, everyone assumed he had killed himself because of grief over the death of his sons—my brothers Robert and John—and because of the loss of all of his wealth, his hundreds of slaves, crops, cattle, sheep, hogs, and all of his money. All that was left were two houses, a few barns, three horses, and thousands of acres of untilled fields in Tennessee and Mississippi that were being steadily overgrown in weeds, briars and scrub pines.

******

My father, Benjamin Lucretius Magruder, was sixty-six when he died. He died on his birthday.

Though five months have passed since Ben found his grandfather's body, he still cries out in his sleep. Ben is only ten. He is my only child.

No one anticipated that my father would commit suicide. With our surrender he was openly bitter and worried about the future, but that was true of all of us. Mama told everyone she had not had the slightest worry about leaving him alone. That morning she had walked across the pike to our house to help Mary, my wife, prepare the dinner and cake for his birthday party. Our homes are four miles south of Columbia, on opposite sides of Pulaski Pike, his on the east side, mine on the west. Our entrances face one another. The houses are set back over two hundred yards from the pike. Together, the two places cover over three thousand acres of the best land in Maury County. He brought us here from Charleston in 1840. The houses are nearly identical: Georgian style, two-story red brick with plain fronts. Kitchens extend to the rear. The old slave quarters are a hundred yards behind the house, the barns beyond. Oaks, maples, tulip poplars shade the houses and lawns. Like the houses, the flower gardens are almost identical in design and planting. Now, uncared for, they, like the fields, are rapidly turning to weeds.

******

The morning of Father's birthday, I saddled my horse and told Mary I was going to Columbia on business but would be back in time to help her and Mama set up for the party. Since a few neighbors had been invited, Father was to be there by five o'clock to greet the guests.

He did not come. At five thirty, guests started arriving. Still he had not come. Everything was ready.

Mama was pacing back and forth in the front hall, ushering everyone into the front parlor to have a glass of dandelion wine. Then she would return to the front door to look down the long, narrow lane to the pike. I could see the wide look growing in her eyes, the look she got when she was starting to get upset. She began to rapidly pat her right thigh—another sign. I watched her out of the corners of my eyes.

She had once been a beautiful woman who loved life, but years of sadness and disappointment had taken their toll. With the deaths of six of her children, her love of life died. When her "people," as she called the slaves, walked away as soon as the Yankees showed up, she could not believe they left her. She had thought they all loved her. Only Old Moll and two or three older ones stayed.

She never looked happy. Even when she smiled it wasn't really a smile; it was little more than a twitch of her lips and cheeks. When anyone spoke to her, she tended to look down or to the side. As I am remembering her, I think of rain clouds or ashes. And there were times when she frightened me. The beginning of her spells had started long ago when we lived in Charleston.

******

By five forty-five all the guests had arrived.

Mama was standing in the opened entrance looking down the lane. "Sometimes he's so un..." Her voice trailed off. Beads of sweat were on her forehead. The pitch of her voice was changing. Her eyes were getting larger. Wisps of hair worked loose onto her forehead. She was rapidly patting her thigh. Since the deaths of my sisters I had seen these signs come upon her—only for days sometimes—but then there were times when she wasn't her real self for a month. My father had no patience with her when she was like this. After loud threats he would order Old Moll—who had been Mama's maidservant since she was a little girl—to take her to the little room at the rear of the house; its walls were thick and the door heavy. It had no window.

Mama looked at the hall clock again, leaned forward, peered into the parlor. Everyone was drinking and talking. She turned and looked at me. Her large eyes stared into mine. They did not blink. "Edmund, you need to go over there and get him," she whispered. Her voice had deepened, as it always did when one of her spells was about to come on her.

But just as she spoke, Mary came out of the parlor and, hearing her, said, "No need to; I've already sent Ben."

And it was at that instant we heard his screams, growing louder and louder, as he came running toward the house, "Mama. . .Mama...Granpa's shot hisself...Granpa's shot hisself!"

******

My father never talked about his parents. Only once did Mama mention them. I don't recall why or when she did. It may have been when I was sitting with her in the little room. I only remember her suddenly saying, "Your father's mother was cruel." That was all.

All I know of his early life is that he was from Scotland and in 1818 shipped from Liverpool to Charleston where he started a sugar store. In a few years he made enough money to become a slave trader, though he always referred to himself as a "broker." Selling Negroes made him wealthy.

In 1825 he built a fine house on the harbor and married Rachael Bondurant, the only daughter of a prominent French Hugenot family in Charleston. She brought him more wealth.

I was born in 1831. Before I was born my father named me Benjamin Edmund Magruder. He was certain I would be a boy. I was to be called "Edmund," the name of his father's father. But when I came, and he saw me as I was, I know he wished I had been stillborn, for he detested all things imperfect and I was more than imperfect. A large red birthmark covers the left side of my forehead, spreading down across my cheek and ear. My left leg is two inches shorter than my right so that I have to wear a built-up shoe and walk with a jerky motion. My speech is slow and hesitant; when I become anxious I stammer so that I appear dull of wit. Nothing about me resembles my father. I am short with small bones and have curly black hair and facial features similar to my mother's. Except for my impairments and her spells, I have always felt that she and I were almost the same person.

Ten months after my birth, mother had another boy but he was dead. Four years later my twin sisters were born and after them in the next five years my brothers, Robert and John, came.

Death lives with our family. In 1841, a yellow fever epidemic killed my pretty little sisters, just as they turned six. Their dying was horrible. I wasn't allowed to go near them so I didn't see it, but Mama told me about it during one of her spells: "My precious little babies were all healthy and happy one day and then they had sweats and headaches and their skin was reddish. Then they turned yellow and vomited, over an' over, and I couldn't stop it and, oh, God, Edmund, streaks of blood ran out of the corners of their eyes and mouths. They suffered continuously for seven days and nights. I didn't leave their sides: cooling them with wet cloths, changing their soiled nightdresses and sheets, reading their favorite stories and praying and begging God to save them. But He didn't...I couldn't understand why He didn't save them. My love for Him should have saved them. And then they died and were buried in the city cemetery.

"Then it came to me—what killed them. I had seen it. The night before my babies first came down with the fever, it came to their room in the dark and stood in the doorway looking into where they lay. It stared at them. It stood there for the longest time with its mouth opening wide, then closing over and over. It was saying something I couldn't hear. It just stood there, staring and moving its lips. I could almost see its face in the candlelight. It was strong looking, tall, straight, and well dressed like a gentleman. For an instant, as it turned from the doorway, its face was clear. I saw that which called itself *Benjamin Lucretius Magruder*. Now, I know it for what it truly is. I know what killed my babies."

******

I never saw a tear in Father's eyes when my sisters died, nor one when they were buried. You would have thought nothing had happened. His face, his voice, his words were, as always, empty of sadness or concern for Mama, much less for me.

I could not stop crying, yet he never dried my tears, never hugged or kissed me. He never said a word. Tears were streaming down Mama's face and he never took her hand. He did not touch us. He did not like to touch or be touched, not even by Mama. He never struck me and I am certain he never struck her. If a slave needed to be whipped, the whipping was given by one of his overseers. While I know of no one, white or Negro, he ever physically hurt, he was the cruelest man I have ever known.

He and Mama slept in separate rooms. Every morning, exactly at four o'clock, he got out of bed. By five o'clock, he had shaved, washed, combed and neatly parted his reddish-brown hair, and dressed in one of his dark suits and weskits tailored in London. The slightest speck of lint was brushed away. His shoes gleamed. He was fastidious in all things: appearance, speech, behavior, and, most especially, in his business dealings.

He was taller than other men, straight and broad-shouldered, with large hands. His body was strong. But it was his cold, deep-set, dark brown eyes, heavy brows, thin lips and sharp-boned face that intimidated anyone who came near him. When he stood before you with his eyes on yours, you did not oppose him—ever.

Once, long ago, as I looked at him, all I saw was darkness and so I have thought of him ever since as darkness.

In public, he presented himself as he wished to be seen: Not as a vulgar, uneducated dealer in human flesh with tobacco juice dripping from the corners of his mouth; but rather, as a man of substance, refined and well-mannered, a man of honor who tithed to the church and was a gentleman of the first order.

His belief was not in God, but in the one who was cast out. I am certain that if he ever prayed it was to that one. As with many things, he deceived others into believing that he was a man of faith. Soon after we arrived in Maury County in 1842, he became a communicant at St. John's Episcopal Church. Religious practices meant nothing to him. He came to church only on Easter and Christmas and then he usually slept through half the service. Once, after an Easter service, I heard Reverend Carpenter ask him, "Mister Magruder, since my sermon today was on the eternal blessings of God upon man, I am interested in your opinion, sir."

Father's face flushed and turned to stone. His eyes narrowed. He looked at Reverend Carpenter for a long moment, as though not comprehending what the reverend had asked, or as if he was looking at a fool. Then he said, "My opinion, sir...my opinion to your exceedingly prolonged sermon about what you call 'the eternal blessings of God'...my opinion, sir, is that I am starving and must get home to eat."

******

After the burial of my sisters, Father left immediately for Savannah with a large coffle of slaves for the market.

The next morning, Mama called me into her bedroom. She was looking into the mirror on her dressing table. She pointed to her right eye.

"Edmund, does this eye look higher than the other one?"

"What?"

"Pay attention! Look at my eyes! Does the right one look higher than the left?"

I leaned forward and looked. “No, ma’am, they both look the same.”

“Oh! Well...well, you go on and eat something. I’m not hungry.”

I did not see her again until that night at the dinner table. She said nothing when she came in and sat down across from me. She laid her Bible beside her napkin. I was so hungry I wasn’t paying any attention to her. Then Old Moll brought in a plate of biscuits but didn’t set them down. She just stood beside Mama looking down at her. I was reaching for the molasses when I realized something was wrong and looked over at Mama. Her forehead was shimmering with sweat. She was staring into the candle flames. At first, I thought the flickering flames were making her eyes tremble. Then, I saw they were flitting back and forth at each of the candles then down at her Bible so quickly that they seemed separate from her. Her lips were moving as though she were speaking but there was no sound.

“Miss Rachael, what’s the matter with you, baby?” asked Old Moll.

Mama didn’t respond. Her eyes continued their rapid movements.

“Mama, look at me! What’s wrong?” I asked loudly.

This time her eyes fixed on mine. For an instant, she did not seem to recognize me. Then, she shook her head and said, “Oh, Edmund, honey, pass me the greens.”

The next day, I was out in the front yard watching ants eat a sparrow I had killed, when she hollered through the open parlor window, "Edmund, come in here for a minute and help me."

As I ran into the room, Old Moll was standing off to the side shaking her head, with her face all knit up as though she was about to cry. Mama was sitting in her rocker, in front of the fireplace, staring into a hand mirror, turning her head, first one way then the other. "Come over here next to me, Edmund...Old Moll keeps telling me I'm wrong, but she can't see worth a hoot anymore. Now, get right up close here and look at my nose."

I leaned against her. She smelled good. She always did. I loved to feel her body touching mine. Some nights, when Father was away, she would let me sleep with her. I would always press myself against her.

She held the mirror closer and touched the right side of her nose. "See how it's bent to the right and looks like it's broken. It makes me look strange...see it right there?"

I squinted and peered at her nose and saw nothing. I stepped back, "Mama, your nose looks just like it always has."

Instantly, her eyes turned angry. She threw the mirror in the fireplace, breaking it to pieces and without a word left the room. That night she did not come down to eat. The next day she seemed herself again. But her face was unhappy.

As the years passed, her "spells" came only once or twice a year. But when they came, they always scared me. During one, she stuffed herself with food. She ate and ate and ate saying, "Oh, I'm so thin." Twice, I saw her stick her fingers down her throat until she vomited. Then, she might fast for days. If I came into her bedroom in the evening, she would turn to me and say, "My precious boy, do you think I'm still a little beauty?"

******

Before my sisters died Mama was called a "petite belle" by her Charleston friends. She was a little bit of a thing, more girl than woman in size. Her face sparkled. Her high voice and smile made everyone but Father smile. Tiny, coal-black curls lay all around her face. When I was a boy I thought of her as a girl. I loved her. As I grew older I loved her more.

But, Ben, you've seen how she was. Unhappiness never left her face, always staring as though she was somewhere else; seldom speaking to any of us; barely attending to her appearance; wandering the house at night, quoting scriptures and praying out loud. Only when she went to church or a funeral would she fix herself up and put on a front as though all was well.

******

In April 1861, Robert and John joined the First Tennessee and left home, never to return. I was given an exemption since I oversaw so many Negroes that were raising cotton and food. There was lots of money to be made during the war. If it hadn't been that he needed me to keep the plantations producing, Father probably would have gotten the army to take me, even with my limp, hoping I would be killed.

A year later, almost to the day of my brothers entering the army, word arrived that John had been killed at Shiloh. The Yankees buried him in a mass grave on the battlefield. My God, the grief that came to Mama and Old Moll. Father was away in Memphis where he was half owner of *Magruder and Powell,* the largest slave brokerage company in Tennessee. Once he was there he usually took a coffle of slaves down to replace those who had died or were worn out on his two plantations in Mississippi. He was gone for three months.

The day after we learned of John's death, Mama came into the library where I was updating Father's account book. Suddenly, she walked over to the desk, closed the book and said, "Edmund, the Devil is doing this to try to get me to curse God."

"What's that, Mama?"

"Taking all my babies away."

I got up and hugged her. "No, Mama, don't say that. It wasn't the Devil; John was killed by the Yankees." I gave her a kiss on the cheek and sat back down. "Now, while I finish up, why don't you go lie down and get some rest."

She reached down and opened the account book, bent over it, squinting her eyes at what was written there. Her eyes moved from left to right, as though she were reading. For a moment, I looked away. When I looked back, she was gone.

******

My brothers were more like Father than Mama. They were handsome, strong and reserved. Early on, Father took them with him to slave sales and to his plantations in Mississippi. They had little to do with me. To them, I was the same as I was to our father, little more than the smartest Negro he owned. I was tutored with them at the house for one year, but come the day of my twelfth birthday, he put me to work in the fields.

When John turned sixteen, he and Robert left for Harvard and I stayed home. If not for Mama's teaching me at night, I would never have learned to read and write or known mathematics well enough to keep the plantation accounts. Though Father instructed her to teach me all I was able to learn, I am certain he did not believe it would be much, for he was convinced I was unable to understand anything complicated.

Except for my ability to drive Negroes in the field and make them work and make money, I was a pariah to him as, increasingly, I was to my brothers who were becoming more and more like him.

Mama was my only refuge. As I grew older, I became more like her, seldom smiling, wondering why God let us be hurt. She began to share her hidden thoughts with me. As I heard them I felt her coming into me. As it grew stronger I began to see and smell and hear and know all that she saw and smelled and heard and knew. One day, as we sat on the bench under the rose arbor, she took my hand and said, "All of this is God's providence to test me as He did Job; He put Satan here, in my house, under my roof."

******

On planting day in the spring of 1844, Father gave me a whip and made me a driver of fifty Negroes. He had been preparing me for this since he first sent me to the fields. For five years, I had worked beside them from dawn until the horn was blown at dusk; I sweated and was dirty and stank like they did. But the day the whip was put in my hand and I was made a driver, it came as easy for me to whip a Negro as it was to whip a mule.

Then, on a sunny summer day on my eighteenth birthday, I was given a chestnut saddle horse to ride beside the overseer, so I could learn his ways: how he worked the fields, cared for the stock, kept the Negroes fit, and oversaw everything necessary to till and plant the land, then harvest it for money.

In 1855, when I was twenty-eight and married, with a new baby—you, Ben—Father named me overseer of all three thousand acres and two hundred and sixty-seven slaves. His giving me that responsibility caused me to believe that one day part of it would be mine. But I should have known that while I gave orders to all those Negroes, I did not own the shadow of a single one of them. Not one thing of all that my father owned would ever be mine—not a house, not a barn, not a horse, cow, or one boll of cotton, not even one small clod of all the clods of dirt that held my sweat.

I discovered this soon after Robert was killed at Nashville in December 1864. Father was away delivering slaves to a plantation outside Montgomery. I had gone to his office to write in the *Slave Birth Register* the names of three children born during the past week. Lying there, on top of the desk, was his will. It was open, as though he wanted me to read it.

And I did. Only then was I convinced that what Mama had been telling me was true. I picked it up and read:

"Be it known that all of my lands, including my two plantations, Glenhaven and Glenmor in Maury County Tennessee, and my two plantations, Glenfernate and Glenbarr in Issaquena County Mississippi, and all of my livestock, farm machinery, crops in the fields and those harvested to be sold; and all of my Negroes; and my half of the brokerage company, Magruder & Powell, in Memphis; and all of my stocks, bonds and money shall go in equal portions to my sons, Robert Disharoon Magruder and John Hamilton Magruder; and that they shall dutifully see to the paying of any and all of my outstanding debts; and that they shall care for my wife, their mother, Rachael Bondurant Magruder, until her death; and that my son, Benjamin Edmund Magruder, and his family shall be allowed to live rent-free in the old overseer's house at Glenmor and that he shall be paid commensurate to his work so long as he faithfully executes his duties.

Written by my hand and witnessed by the two signatories below my name on this May 17, 1861.

Benjamin Lucretius Magruder
Witnessed by:
Thomas Finch
James Syler

Below this, in his hand writing, is the following addition:

Be it known now that as my sons Robert Disharoon Magruder and John Hamilton Magruder have both died in the war, I now by this addendum to my will make it known that it is my wish that Robert Edward Magruder, son of Robert Disharoon Magruder, and that James Calhoun Magruder, son of John Hamilton Magruder, shall receive all of my land, slaves, houses, livestock, and all other of my possessions in the same equal portions as their fathers would have had they lived; and that they shall see to the care of my wife, Rachael Bondurant Magruder, and son, Benjamin Edmund Magruder, as defined in my will of May 17, 1861.

So written by my hand on January 24, 1865.

Benjamin Lucretius Magruder
Witnessed by:
Thomas Finch
James Syler

As I read, I smelled the sulphur from his mouth. It rose from the paper. I blew my nose and spat on the floor. I had never believed in demons for I did not believe one word of the Bible; it was all superstition, made up by men who made their living creating tales to explain the awfulness of life and how the next life would be better if you gave them money. But Mama taught me I was wrong, for she had seen a demon, had touched it, smelled it, and taken it into herself. And over time, as I listened to her, there came into me images and sounds like those within her. As I reread the will I realized that all that she had been telling me was true—and that a demon was living among us.

******

The day after she learned John had been killed at Shiloh, Mama began taking laudanum morning, noon, and night. Mostly, it calmed her. But when Robert was killed in Nashville two years later, it was little better than water. She wandered from room to room, praying loudly, over and over, "Dear God, protect me from the evil one, cast him out into the fire, save me from the roaring lion...slay the serpent." Some days this went on for hours. Afterwards, she slept half a day, sometimes the entire day.

The old Negroes still on the place after Robert's death, were so scared of her they avoided coming to the house; if they had to, they never looked at her face, especially her eyes. Only Old Moll could comfort her. If Father happened to be here, he had her give Mama laudanum until she passed out. He couldn't tolerate her spells. A few weeks before his birthday, he had a doctor come from Columbia to examine her. The doctor said she had *religious monomania* and should be put in the asylum in Nashville, but as it was occupied by the Yankees the only thing that could be done was to increase the laudanum when she became too excited. And if she became uncontrollable, he told Father to lock her up somewhere where she couldn't hurt herself or escape.

Three nights after Robert's death, Father sent a Negro over to tell me to come quick and help him with Mama.

He was standing in the open front door when I tied my horse to the post by the porch. As I limped up the steps he snapped, "Damnit, boy, can't you move any faster than that?" Without answering, I stepped inside the entrance hall as he continued, "She's in the parlor and has wrapped her arms around my Grandfather clock and says she'll pull it over if I try to take her out...Dr. Lester's right, she's crazy as she can be and needs to be put away but, until we can, I want her locked up in that back room. Now you get in here and help Old Moll!"

I did. I gently gripped Mama's arms. She resisted for a moment, then gave way to Old Moll and me patting her and telling her we loved her and that everything would be all right. We took her to the small room off the kitchen. The thick walls and door muffled her loud praying and pleading. When we were finished, Father gave the keys to Old Moll and said, "If she gets out you'll be sorry."

******

Every night after that, when I left the fields, I went to see Mama. Usually, toward nightfall she calmed. We would talk. Then, in that little cramped room on a steamy August night, she suddenly said, "He sleeps with Negroes. He's done it since the day we were married." She told it matter-of-factly, as though she were talking about something she had read in a novel. But she was speaking of her husband, my father. For a moment I couldn't comprehend it but then I knew, as she touched my cheek, that it was true for she never lied to me. I felt such a terrible sadness for her and—after the sadness—there came a great hatred for my father.

A few evenings later, as I entered her room, her eyes were wide and her hand was rapidly patting her thigh. She jumped from her bed and gripped my hands and said, "Edmund, do you know there are demons in him? Do you want to know how they got into him?" The words rushed from her, as she struck her thigh as fast as her hand would go. "They came from all those Negroes he's laid with. You know how they worship demons from where they come from. And...and...you know how he hates to get dirt on himself...well, he'd come in with dirt on his hands and knees from where he'd been laying on one of them out in the fields. I've seen it...I've seen it...I've seen the dirt as black as they were on his knees and hands, and I could smell their stink on him...Lord God, the stink. You know those people aren't human like us, they've got demons inside of them. That's how they got in him. They entered him when he was on top of them. They came up in his thing. No telling how many he's got in him."

As she talked, I could see what she saw; I could see what had been beyond my understanding. As I listened, her words came into me and became part of me; all that had been was revealed—all those years since the ones I could first remember—when my father shunned me, when he had not loved me and would never love me. All those years, I had been able to believe it was only because I was not made right, that all of me was an ugliness he could not bear. And because of what was revealed, I knew that nothing that was his would ever be mine. Nothing. Nothing. Especially his love.

To protect himself, he would have put Mother away from sight forever—for she knew who he really was.

******

Ben, you probably wonder why I have not said more about your mother. I can only say it is because I know little about her other than she is a good woman and keeps God's commandments. We are so different. The only thing we share is our love for you. I am comforted knowing she will raise you to be a good man.

I had hoped that killing my father would have killed the demons and protected you, but it is not yet dead. This morning when I was shaving, I saw in the mirror that my birthmark is gone and my hair has turned reddish-brown. I spoke to the mirror. My stammer is gone. That which was in my father is growing in me. It will soon become me, as it did with Mama. I have killed that one in her. Now, my dear mother will never be locked away. I am sorry Old Moll tried to stop me. I no longer trust myself. Father's derringer lies on the desk in front of me. It will now destroy the last one.

Goodbye, Ben.

I love you.

Benjamin Edmund Magruder
November 17, 1865

THE TWIN

It is cold. Snow is falling all across the barrens. It began at noon; soon after the Twin tried to kill him. He is frightened. Blood is splattered over his face, hands, clothes, and boots; it is almost frozen. Its smell mixes with the mustiness of the thicket that surrounds his hunkered form. His breath wisps into the cold, dimming air. His eyes scan back and forth for movement in the woods for the slightest shift of a shadow. He holds his shotgun across his knees.

The thicket hedges the side of the narrow road that runs along the bottom of the deep, wooded hollow. The rutted water in the road is frozen. A small bird flits down into a rut, pecks twice at the ice, then flares up and away into the trees.

The light is fading. The hill's long shadow has begun to cover him. Soon the rabbits will come out onto the road. He is hungry. He cocks the hammer of the twelve-gauge. It makes a dull click.

He holds his breath and listens. Something moves on the hill behind him, a faint crunching of twigs. He is ready. His knife is sharp. His pockets are crammed with shells.

A low rumble comes from the west, lights flash against the dark clouds. Across the road, a form moves through the trees. It disappears, appears again then disappears. He looks closely at the edges of the tree trunks and into their shadows. The form is gone.

There is a whiff of smoke and blood in the air. His nostrils spread; his chest rises and falls. He takes deep breaths, seeking the source, a hint of the Twin. He is frightened. Had he dug a hole for protection, the snow would have covered the fresh turned earth.

He raises the shotgun from his knees, places the butt against the ground, slowly tilts the barrels upward and slants the muzzles toward his chin. He looks at the woods and into them. Nothing is there. He moves the shotgun back across his knees.

Now, as darkness comes, the air is clean and colder. The road is almost covered with snow. He smiles. He cannot be seen. The Twin does not know he is here. Though he is cold, he will not move.

It is almost time for the rabbits to leave their hiding places and come out onto the road. Hunger sharpens his ears for sounds on the hills around him; his eyes quicken for movement in the woods.

From beyond the hill, at the end of the hollow, an echo like the distant baying of hounds comes and goes – comes and goes – comes and goes, each time nearer, louder, until, just above the trees – a flight of geese come fast over the hill, through the snow, and are gone.

Darkness fills the hollow. Night is almost here. The time has come. Soon, very soon, the Twin will leave his hiding place. Cautiously, silently, he will leave the woods and come out onto the road where his tracks will be quickly covered by the falling snow.

BLOOD FOR BLOOD

There are still people in the mountains who believe I am a witch, who believe that I once floated across Lost Cove's floodwaters in an eggshell, that I cast a spell on a sawmill and made the saw run backwards, and that I have the power of Satan to cause sickness and death. When I come upon them in the stores in Sewanee and Sherwood they turn their faces and those of their children away from me. When I greet them they never speak. Sixty years ago, these kinds of people frightened me. But not now.

In the summer of 1829, a hard drought came to the mountains. Not a drop of rain fell. When it hung on into the next year, worries turned to fear; with some, the fear turned to anger and to the beginning of rumors that a curse was upon the land that the Devil had come among them.

It was then that they began to search for witches. God's commandment directed them - *Thou shalt not suffer a witch to live.*

This evil commandment led to murder.

Many things have been done in the name of the Lord that have brought evil, for His book is filled with both lies and great truths. *The Lord giveth and the Lord taketh away*, is one. I know this one to be true for He did both to me. He gave me life. He gave me the gift of healing. He gave me the second sight. Most of all, he gave me Mama Osie and William. But he took away my parents. He took away something inside of me so that I could never have children. He gave me a thick tongue and took away the clarity of my speech. He created me so that others think I am strange. His book also says, "Blessed be the name of the Lord." But I cannot bring myself to bless Him.

On the day I was born I became an orphan. My father, who gave me my red hair, was killed that morning by a British musket ball at New Orleans. That evening, my mother hemorrhaged to death on the ground after having me beside a spring at the head of Roark's Cove.

By the time night came, both of my parents were dead. If Mama Osie had not been there, I would have been dead too. She pulled me from my mother's body. She tore the veil from my face. She cut the cord, tied it with horsehair, lifted me to her mouth, and breathed life into me. She poured water from the spring over me until I shook and cried. Then she wrapped me in a bobcat's skin and carried me over the mountain to her cabin in Lost Cove.

She was young and lived alone when I was born. She raised me as if I had come from inside her. As I grew older, she told me who my real mother was and that my eyes were just like hers, "black as tha night." She taught me all she knew about this world and the underworld and the world that was to come. With her Bible, she taught me to read and write; and in the fields and woods, I learned which plants and roots healed, which were poisonous; and when kidding time came for the goats, she taught me how to deliver babies. Except for William, she is the only person who has ever kissed me or said to me, "I love you."

"Mama," for indeed she became my mama, was a tall, strongly-built Cherokee with high, rounded cheekbones, a narrow forehead, thin lips, a round nose, skin the color of dark chestnut and shiny black hair and eyes. Three purple tattooed lines ran from the center of her lower lip down into the cleft of her chin.

On the first day of every week she sprinkled red earth onto her hair and tied red and blue bird feathers into the long strands that hung down her back. She dressed in red-and-green-dyed muslin dresses, goatskin moccasins and leggings, and smoked a small stone pipe shaped like a panther. She prayed daily to the Christian God and to the spirits who live in the upper and lower worlds.

When I was old enough to understand, she told me my visions were a gift and that I must keep my heart and body clean for the visions to come to me. Even now, the first thing I do every morning, is pour a cup of water over my body and say my prayers of thanks to all the spirits.

Mama was so kind and gentle, no one would have believed she could ever have killed someone.

Only once did she speak of what our people call, 'the taking of blood for blood.' We had finished eating supper and were sitting by the fire. I was weaving a basket when she suddenly said, "I kilt a man when I wus bout yer age. He'd kilt my Papa in an argument over a horserace. After we buried Papa, I waited four months. Then one mornin, when there was a heavy mist near tha ground, I got up in tha dark an filled a pack with food, a blanket, an a knife, an a gourd of water an walked all tha way down tha valley ta where tha killer lived. I member tha mornin light was all milky when I hid inside his barn an waited til he come ta feed his mule. When he stepped inside tha barn door, I stuck a pitchfork in im three times. Then I run through tha woods ta tha old trail that went north into tha mountains – six days of hard runnin an walkin got me to tha cove. I wus starvin an couldn go on when I seen a house an went up ta hit an asked for some food. They fed me an let me sleep in tha barn. So that's how I come ta live yhar an I never went back. Those folks were tha Garners...Years later, when I heerd my mama an my lil sister had died from tha rain an cold while tha Army was movin all our people away, I could have kilt Jackson jest as easy as I kilt my Papa's killer." When she finished, she rolled over on her side and said, "That's hit." She never spoke of the killing again.

Most of my beliefs and most of my ways are those she taught me, but there our likeness ends. I'm not more than half her size; and now I'm old. I'm getting smaller every year, yet I'm still agile and can go up and down the mountains almost as fast as a goat. My skin is fair and covered with freckles. My long red hair has faded and is streaked with gray; sometimes I tie crow and hawk feathers into it. I wear tattered men's coats and pants and floppy hats I make from goatskins. Above my right breast is a sun and moon and above my left are five stalks of corn; Mama tattooed them after I had my first vision. When I look at them in a mirror, I glimpse her just for a moment, carefully pricking my skin, trying her best not to hurt me.

Our old cabin is steadily falling apart, but I continue to live in it for its comfort of memories. It sits on a rise at the north end of the cove, higher than the cove has ever flooded. The dirt floor has been packed hard by humans and goats. The log walls and cedar shingles are crisscrossed with a patchwork of boards that cover cracks and rot. It smells of goats, smoke, grease, dried herbs, honey, and crow droppings. Herbs, roots, animal skins and clothes hang from the low ceiling beams. Sitting in the corners are woven honeysuckle baskets filled with corn, potatoes, dried fruits and nuts; beside them are clay pots where I keep my curdled goat's milk and muscadine wine. In the fireplace, on a flat stone, is a large iron pot with raised letters on its side that read, "Wilkinson Iron Works - 1790." Old Mr. Silas Garner told me once that he thought the pot came from the old country.

There is a hole in the mud chinking by the front door. I made it for my pet crow, "Chief James Vann." I call him "Jamie." He comes and goes as he pleases to and from his flock that roost in the trees behind the cabin. I took him from a nest when he was little and split his tongue to help him talk; he says a few words, "Haw, Haw - Bye, Bye - Maw, Maw" and can say my name almost as I do, "Maw-ee - Mae-ee." Even to me it sounds funny. I named him after a Cherokee chief who might have saved our people's lands if he hadn't been shot to death in a revenge killing. He was sipping whiskey when the Minnie ball struck him.

During the first summer Mama lived in the cove, she saved the life of one of the Garner girls who'd been struck by a timber rattler. Kindred Garner, the girl's father, gave his thanks to Mama with a billy and two nanny goats. They were the start of her herd. She loved them, named them, talked to them like they were people; she drank their milk and ate them and wore their skins. She told me once that the Great Spirit wouldn't have given them to us just to play with. Before cutting their throats, she always sprinkled corn meal over their heads and backs and then she thanked them for what they were giving her.

It was goat's milk that saved my life when I was a baby. As I grew older, goats were my only playmates. By the time I was five I could speak their language, yet I could not say one human word anyone but Mama could understand. By eight, I could howl and screech, whistle and growl like most of the animals and birds that lived in the cove; but when I said, "Mama," it came out "Maa-ahhh."

I cannot speak clearly, but I see things others cannot.

In the north field, there is a stone shaped like a coffin lid. It lies near the giant tulip tree, a hundred strides from the door of the cabin. The head of the stone points east. There are carvings on it made by the old ones: a sun and moon and five stalks of corn exactly like the ones above my breasts. In the middle of summer, when the sun is directly overhead, the stone shines like silver. The stone fits my back perfectly. That is where I lie to watch the clouds shift their shapes. It is where I see visions.

When the days are splendid, when breezes make waves on the long grass, when the forest is dark green and the sky is blue and the clouds pure white, I may lie on the stone for half a day watching the clouds turn into faces and angels and animals and sometimes into things that are to come.

It was there, sitting on the stone, that I had my first vision. I was twelve. The nannies were dropping their kids, and I was there if they needed help. They were all around me in the field, some lying down, others nibbling on grass. Now and then one called to me or to the others, "nahaaaaa," and be answered, "nahaaaaa." Israel, the bearded, curved-horn billy, slept in the shade of the tulip tree. I was drying a just-born kid with sedge when a large shadow passed over. I looked up just as an eagle glided above us. It was close enough I could see its eyes staring at me, it gave a long, rasping scream and veered upward, flapping its wings; it rose higher and higher until it was far up in the sky, where it began circling. Each time, as it passed before the sun, I lost sight of it – then it was gone.

I laid the kid on the ground, stood up and searched the sky. My eyes burned and watered from staring into the sun. I squeezed them shut, then looked again. Where the eagle had been there was a dark mass of clouds growing larger and larger; it moved in and out of itself, changing shape as though it were alive. Suddenly the center opened and formed itself into a mouth filled with lightning and fiery teeth covered in black blood. Its tongue was made of whips, each with the head of a snake that was singing, *Holy, Holy, Holy, Lord God Almighty*, over and over, then there came a mighty wind and a voice that rumbled like thunder from deep in the mouth's throat saying, *There shall come a day when I shall smite them with rods and I shall burn their land with fire.* Then it was gone, and the sky was clear.

I was so terrified for a second I couldn't move; then I ran to the cabin and told Mama what I'd seen.

She said nothing for a long moment, she stared at me; it was like she was looking at someone other than me. Then her face looked normal again, and she said, "Well hits happen, ye've had a foretellin of somethin that's ta come...hit's a warnin from God that somethin bad is comin."

That night she pored a whole jug of water on herself and on me, and we both prayed to God and the spirits to protect us.

But they didn't. The badness came on us that summer.

In the second year of the drought, people began to say that the end of the world was at hand and that God had turned His Face from us because of our sinful ways. Nonbelievers gathered with believers to pray for rain and forgiveness. But the drought continued. When summer came, the air turned to fire. Creeks and springs dried up. Earth became dust. Cattle and crops died. Birds fell from trees. Without help from their neighbors, old people who had no family would have died. Our garden never came. The spring slowed to a trickle. The nannies had no milk and three kids were born dead. We survived on the food stored in our root cellar. We ate most of our goats. We shared what we could with the Pearsons and Garners, as they did with us.

When people's prayers were not answered and no rain came, the whispers and accusations began. Among them were some who feared and hated Indians, who believed they could never be trusted, that they were not like white people, that they worshipped demon spirits and practiced witchcraft. Soon, they started to talk against Mama, though she had helped almost every family within a day's walk of our cabin. As the drought stretched on, the accusations began that she was a witch; that she was the one who had put a curse on the land, and that she slept with the Devil and that I was their child. And then it was that someone said we should both be killed AS God had commanded.

And so they came to kill us.

Mama was killed on the first day of August, 1829, by Green Pullen and his younger brother, Bob. She'd left the cabin early that morning carrying a bag of potatoes and goat jerky to old Miss Gudger who lived by herself a half mile this side of Sewanee.

Mama was on her way home and had just come under the natural bridge. They were waiting for her.

They killed her, piled brush on her body and burned her. Then they came for me.

I was with the goats at the spring in the woods behind the cabin. It was cooler there. We were dozing in the small clearing when the crows in the trees above us began making loud warning calls. Israel gave a quick, hoarse snort, jumped to his feet, and turned to face the footpath to the cabin. The other goats were immediately standing and alert, their noses and ears twitched as they looked toward the footpath. The oldest nanny stomped the ground hard with her left front hoof, signaling danger. I sat up and looked down the trail with my hands cupped behind my ears and listened.

The voices of the Pullens came up the footpath. Mama had warned me about them, "Don't ya ever let them Pullens git near ya when yer alone. They hate us an they'll hurt ya if they ever get hold of ya."

I'd seen the hate in their eyes when they passed us on the road or at the store in Sewanee; they'd spit on the ground and make a cross with their fingers and curse, "Goddamn ye, ye'd best git outta these hyar mountains."

Now they were almost at me, I was terrified. I got up without a sound. The goats moved closer to me; Israel's shoulder pressed against my leg. The Pullen's voices were just around the bend from the clearing when I began running up the mountain. The herd was right behind me. Halfway up, the goats left me, one by one. Israel was the last. I didn't stop until I reached the top.

Thirty years later, in the fall of 1860, shortly after William died, I returned to Lost Cove. Three weeks after my return, both of the Pullen brothers were found dead on the same day: Bob burned to death in his barn. Green was found hanging in the woods behind his house.

On April 12, 1861, the lightning and fire I had seen in the sky when I was twelve years old came down upon the South. It did not end for four years.

HALLOWEEN 1946

And lead us not into temptation, but deliver us from evil.
For thine is the kingdom, and the power, and the glory forever. Amen
Matthew 6:13

But the Good Lord didn't deliver us! In fact, He's the One ultimately responsible for Halloween. He's the One who approved the Devil's request to create a day "just 'especially for young boys and criminals." He's the one that backed the Devil up in setting October 31 as Halloween every year to scare the bejesus out of us. Somewhere in the Bible He admits it, "Know ye this, I created Halloween with the Devil's help to scare the hell out of you so ye would turn from your evil ways and turn back to Me to save your evil soul from the fiery depths."

Serious studies have been done by the Church of the Revelations in Hohenwald, Tennessee that prove - beyond all dispute - Halloween has brought multitudes of lost sinners back to the Lord. As always, we, the Cherokee Five, did our part to help Him out.

Think about this for a moment: five boys, ages 10 to 14, their faces covered with masks, roaming your neighborhood on Halloween night. It sort of gets your "on guards" perked up with thoughts of, *What'n hell kinda awfulness are they planning before this night's over.*

Billy Bob wore a bright, red Devil's mask that had hair like little flames coming out the sides and top. It must have cost a bundle 'cause it 'ud scare the you know what out of little children and scary types of grown ups.

TC thought he looked just like King Kong with his big black-faced gorilla mask. His neck got red and he clenched his fist when I said, "Doggone it TC, you're a perfect monkey."

Double M said he was a goat but when he bleated through his mask he sounded like his throat was being cut.

Bush slipped his mask on and made a pretty good roaring sound which was supposed to be a grizzly. The only problem was the mask looked more like Lassie.

Mine was home made with bits and pieces of paper and cloth put together with scotch tape, strings and big rubber bands and painted all over. When I put it on, Billy Bob stepped back and grimaced, "The Lord have mercy, GE, what...what's that?"

"I'm gonna be a Crazy Clown." First, I'd painted the whole thing white, then put big red lips and cheeks in a smile like the Joker's. The eyes were coal-black with large arching eyebrows. I liked what I saw in the mirror so I added a scar that came down from my left forehead, across my eye, ending below my cheek. When

I came out of the bedroom my sisters screamed and ran out of the room and our dog tried to crawl under the couch – I knew I was ready.

We set out as it was turning from dusk to dark. All our parents told us to be home by 10:00 or they would come looking for us and several of them hinted at beatings if we did anything that might lead to neighbors threatening lawsuits or the police showing up with blue lights flashing.

We gathered in Billy Bob's backyard. Except for Bush carrying a silly plastic pumpkin bucket, the rest of us had brown grocery bags to put our treats in.

"OK guys, let's go get 'em," said Billy Bob.

We cut through the backyard hedge and the yard beyond to a brightly lit front porch of an old two-story house where we were greeted at the door by two obnoxious teenage boys who immediately began making fun of us. When Billy Bob blurted out "Trick or treat," the oldest one laughed, "Well treat this trick up yours," and shot us a finger and slammed the door in our face.

That was a big mistake.

Without a word we followed Billy Bob back around the house to the backyard to the goldfish pond with its concrete statue of a sweet, little child standing in the center. One after another we ringed ourselves around the pond, unzipped our pants, pulled ourselves out and pissed every drop of piss we had in us outward as far as we could go. It glittered in the moonlight. TC and

Double M were our champion pissers. Both hit the statue. Someone must have struck a big goldfish right between its eyes, for it wasn't a second before one turned belly-up onto the surface.

After this, most people were nice, filling our bags with candy and cookies and one lady even gave us a slice of pecan pie. We went out to the street, curved our bottoms down in a ditch and gorged: pie first, cookies second, ending with Goo Goos for desert. Then everyone got silent and laid back and looked up at the stars. "Damn, that's pretty," somebody muttered.

"Damn right 'bout that," said someone else.

"Wonder what's up there?" asked Bush.

"Hell Bush, don't they teach you anything at all at that St. whatever place it is you go to on Sunday? God's up there and heaven too."

"But where up there? All I can see are stars."

"I guess beyond 'em somewhere. Damn Bush, ask one of those Catholic guys that wears sheets an all that fancy stuff...Yeh see Bush, that's one of the problems with Catholics, ya'll only sprinkle a little water on a baby's head an don't really dunk people all the way down under the water to the bottom when yeh baptize 'em...no wonder ya'll don't know doodly-squat 'bout God an heaven an stuff. Plus yeh have to eat fish every Friday 'til yeh die...Can't yeh see somethin' ain't right?"

Suddenly, Billy Bob jumped to his feet and out of the ditch announcin', "OK guys, it's gettin' on an' we got a bunch more houses to hit before goin' home...Let's go!"

No one was home in the next two houses so we hung their porch chairs up in trees. At the next door a little rat-like dog came growling out and grabbed ahold of my left pants leg and wouldn't let go. The beast's owner was a nice old lady who told him, "Stop that Hubbert, leave that nice boy alone," and picked him up and gave me an extra Hershey bar and a pat on the head.

We saved Brother Black's house for last. He was a preacher and teacher made out of flint and had turned us away once when we asked to put a lost pony we'd caught into his pasture. We'd fixed him then and I was ready to do it again if he acted like a craphead.

Every light was off. I knocked. No lights came on. No one opened the door. I knocked again - still nothing. "OK, let's all knock." We did - Nothing.

"OK, bang on it as hard as you can an' holler trick or treat as loud as you can."

We banged away and hollered, **"TRICK OR TREAT...TRICK OR TREAT...TRICK OR TREAT!"**

Suddenly the door flew open.

He stood there with a face of stone glaring down on us like the wrath of God. So he thought...so he thought. I stared upward straight into his eyes thinking, *'You ain't God. All you are is a mean old Craphead.'*

Still he stood there – silent - staring at us. Then, he raised his left arm with his hand toward our faces, "Get thee behind me you little Satans!" And flicked his fingers at us as though we were insects and slammed the door so quick and hard he hit Bush's pumpkin bucket and cracked it, spilling candy everywhere.

We stood for a long moment almost bleeding from the corner of our eyes we were so angry. "Let's kill 'im," said Double M who liked Edward G. Robinson gangster movies.

"Un un, I brought somethin' for him," and pulled two strong clothesline cords out of my pocket and stretched them out tightly, "These 'ul fix old Craphead."

"Damn GE, I didn't really mean for us ta kill 'im."

"Ya'll follow me an' be quiet." I led them through the dark, opened the gate to the field and walked slowly toward the dark outlines of Black's four walking-horses as I reached into my sack and got some chocolate out.

The horses smelled it and came toward me. "Bush, get some chocolate and feed it to them while I go behind them an' do somethin'."

After I'd finished tying the horse's tails together I whispered, "OK, let's go home."

That night I slept the sleep of the righteous.

GOD'S PUNISHMENT

Hear the word of the Lord God as it is written in Numbers 14:18, *The Lord is longsuffering, and of great mercy, forgiving iniquity and transgression, and by no means clearing the guilty, visiting the iniquity of the fathers upon the children into the third and fourth generation.*

My name is Nancy Mae Pearson. My grandchildren call me "Nanny." I am eighty years old. Every night before I get into bed I ease down on my knees and ask the Lord for forgiveness and for His mercy to take away my sins from those who come after me. Guilt weighs heavy on me for what I did long ago, things I have never told to anyone, things that brought terrible suffering upon my family. Now, I have decided I must tell them before I die so that they all will be warned and may have the strength I did not and, the Lord willing, will avoid bringing pain upon their own.

Of my nine children, only Lillie Jane, my daughter, and Jeremiah, her husband, and I remain here in Lost Cove where it all happened. Everyone else is dead. Nathaniel Pearson, my husband, and six of our babies are buried in the cemetery a little ways back of the house on the lower slope of the mountain. One day, I will lie there beside Nathaniel, and near my babies:

Tennessee, who like my unnamed first child, never took a breath of life; James, who we called "Brother", our first live born, was killed with his father; Patty, a straight-laced old maid school teacher; Lafe, our second son, though strange and sometimes scary, may have had within himself the most love of us all; and our little one, "Angel," who we thought of as sent down from above. Jane Ann is buried with her husband in Nashville in the Catholic cemetery and Betty Sue disappeared with her husband somewhere, far out on the plains in Indian country.

I could not write my name until I was sixty-eight. Then Lillie Jane said it was time for me to learn and she would teach me. She was a good teacher and every night, after supper, I was her student. She taught me to read and write and spell. I have practiced all that I learned, over and over and over for years, and now, in my old age, I have confidence in myself that what I write will be as it should be and that my confession will make clear why we must heed God's warnings and, if we do not, how His punishment can descend upon those we love.

Before I married I was a Wagner. Mama and Daddy and the ten of us children lived on Crow Creek, a mile or so down from Buggy Top Cave. We came from North Carolina in 1839, the year after Jackson rounded up the Cherokees and sent them west. Mama said I was born when they were halfway here. She said they were on top of a mountain when her water broke and they had to stop for three hours while she had me in the midst of a thunderstorm. I wonder if that is what marked me. For truth be known, I was an ugly baby and never got any better. As long as I can remember seeing myself in a mirror I have seen someone looking back at me who is as ugly as homemade sin, but then, thank God, I was born tough and I was born smart, at least smart most of the time.

When we finally got to our eighty acres on Crow Creek Mama said Daddy swore terribly bad, for a good bit better than half of our land was a steep mountain slope and the rest, more rock than dirt. As the old saying goes, "We were as poor as Job's turkey" and could barely make a go of it. Six of us were girls. I was the youngest. As soon as one of us turned twelve, Daddy began to look for any man, no matter his age, who would take us off his hands. Mama never argued against him on this or, for that matter, on anything else. So, one after the other, my sisters were taken off. When I turned twelve I was the only one left.

For me, twelve turned to twenty and I was still there. My going took eight more years. I guess it was being as ugly as I was that caused no one to want me. But my time finally came. I have always believed it came about because Daddy gave Nathaniel Garner real money to marry me. The day we walked out of church I saw Daddy give Nathaniel a ten dollar gold piece.

We married the summer of 1858. I did not love Nathaniel. I loved his wild brother Silas and, though Silas was married, I lay with him one last time in Buggy Top Cave the week before my wedding while Nathaniel was away in Winchester for a mule sale.

No matter my face and the money, I could tell that Nathaniel was truly taken with me the morning after our first night together. I knew I was good at making love; Silas had told me so four times. Poor Nathaniel, he never suspicioned the baby girl born dead eight months after we married was not his. She was not fully formed. We never named her. It will be on my heart until I die. That poor little thing bore the retribution for my sin of fornication, but she did not bear it away forever; for it returned two-fold the next year when Angel and Lafe were born. Both were born alive but each one, in its own way, was not created whole.

We all liked to say that Angel came to us made of love. You could see it in her face and hear it in her sounds even though she could not speak or take a step and her body being so small and twisted. She loved us, as we loved her, everyday of her fourteen years.

At first, Lafe seemed normal but then, when he had just turned four, God sent more retribution on us. On November 17, 1864, John Gaunt and his band of Rebel Bushwhackers rode down the mountain into the cove and tortured and hanged Nathaniel and Brother for hiding runaway slaves. They were slaughtered like hogs. And, Oh God, Lafe was forced to watch and hear it all. The horror of it never left him, and as the years passed his soul became twisted more than Angel's body.

The loss of my baby and my husband who I had grown to love...my Lord, the pain has never left me; I know now that it never will leave me. As I washed and dressed their bodies, hatred came slowly into me until it filled me. I swore to God that, when the time was at hand, I would, as He had with me, take my vengeance, even though He had said, "Vengeance is mine." There was no forgiveness left in me. Every night I lay in bed seeing what I would do. I know I may be damned to hell forever for the hatred that consumed me. I did not try to stop it. I did not pray, "Father, forgive them for they know not what they do." I prayed for their deaths. So I waited for the time to come the Cherokees called, "The taking of blood for blood." Then I would take my revenge.

And the time did come. On December 23, 1864, a week after the Battle of Nashville, the cold fell hard across the mountains. Icicles hung from the nostrils and lips of mules and cows; water froze in buckets beside the fire; snow lay knee deep on the ground; tree limbs popped like rifle shots. The clouds hung low and dark above the cove all that day. Night came. The children were asleep in the loft. I was sitting in my rocker in front of the fireplace mending the girl's dresses when there was a knock at the door. Quietly, I got up and took Nathaniel's loaded rifle down from above the fireplace and went to the door and asked who was there. A boy's voice answered.

Standing there in the dim light were two boys, both dressed in ragged butternut uniforms. Their dirty, gaunt faces and deep set eyes showed their fear; they had no weapons; they were just two freezing, starving boys who had fought and lost with Hood in Franklin and Nashville and now, tired of fighting, they had slipped away from the Confederate Army and were headed home to their mamas and papas and sisters and brothers in Georgia.

They had lost their way. With no food and no heavy coats or blankets they were slowly freezing to death. When they came upon the natural bridge at the north end of the cove, they walked out on it and saw, far below, smoke rising from our chimney. They followed it to our house.

They were polite boys. Holding their hats in their hands, saying "Yes Mam" and "No Mam," you could tell their mamas had taught them good manners. Neither one was more than four or five years older than Brother when John Gaunt killed him. All they asked for was for permission to sleep in the barn. They did not ask for food.

I brought them inside, warmed them by the fire and fed them. When they were full I gave them heavy wool blankets; lit the coal-oil lantern and led them to the barn; put fresh straw in a stall and told them to come to the house in the morning for breakfast. The smallest had tears in his eyes as he thanked me. He said I reminded him of his mama.

I waited two hours to be sure they were asleep, then I got the ax from behind the wood box and went straight to the barn and killed them both. I put their bodies in the wagon and covered them with hay. The next morning I told the children I was going to the Big Sink to get more dead limbs for firewood. When I got there I dumped the bodies into the Sink.

Killing them did not take away my pain. It brought more.

God's punishment came again upon me and on my family for the hatred in my heart and for the killing of those two innocent boys. Lafe, my only living son, was chosen once more. In the winter of 1878, John Gaunt shot him to death on the road between Sherwood and Sewanee. Moments later, Lafe's fourteen-year-old friend, Jeremiah Vann, killed John Gaunt.

Long years passed. Jeremiah married Lillie Jane. He has become a son to me. They have five children. In my nightly prayer I plead with God to not hurt them for my sins and that He will be merciful unto them, and that my death, when it comes, will be sufficient to remove my iniquities from my grandchildren and great grandchildren forever. Amen.

Nancy Mae Pearson
Lost Cove
January 1919

THE WHIPPOORWILL CALLS AT NIGHT

Night has come since the tall man began digging and now he stands in an open grave as deep as his chest, slowly swinging a mattock partway up then down into the brown-red earth, the blade cutting into the ground over and over without a pause. Above him, a pine torch burns on top of the mound of fresh dirt heaped beside the grave. With each swing of the mattock, the air ripples the flame's yellow wave, flickering light down into the hollows of his face and onto the crusty stains that cover his hands and wrists.

It is late summer. The air is hot and sticky; the rain clouds that came from the southwest at noon are completely covering the Barrens, blocking all moon and starlight from the mountains and valleys. Midway into this vast wilderness is a long L shaped cove. A small creek runs through it. Beside the creek, at the upper end of the cove, there is a rough, half-cleared field, a strip of rocky soil covered with tree stumps and dry corn stubble. The grave is here, between the field and the creek, beneath a giant tulip tree.

The tall man is not old, though his stiff half-movements are as those of the old, or of someone who is ill, or injured. His skin is stretched tight over the sharp bones of his face. He is leathery and angular, with long, coal-black hair and beard that are matted and greasy. His overalls hang like an empty sack, filthy with sweat and dirt and black matter. He has not eaten or slept for three days. At dusk, just as the sun began to drop behind the mountain, he felt his shadow beginning to separate and slip away. Now, from deep in their sockets, his eyes dully watch formations of light and dark on the walls of the grave, they swirl together, then part and rise upward into the air and through the flame into the tree branches and the night beyond, where they disappear.

At that instant a whippoorwill calls; and before it ends, he hears another from across the field - then another - and another - and another. He does not move; he holds the mattock above his head, then lowers it slowly to his chest, lays it beside the mound, picks up a wooden bowl behind his feet, and begins to scoop the loose soil from the bottom of the grave which he tosses onto the mound and thinks,

Thank God hit are dun, hit are dun.

When there is no more loose dirt, he pitches the bowl beside the mattock and heaves himself up and over the side of the grave onto the ground. He sits there, breathing hard, exhausted, staring into the dark, then closes his eyes and leans forward and clasps his arms around his legs, resting his forehead on his bent knees and listens. Across the field, towards the cabin he hears her calling,

Do ye hyar our purties singing, do ye hyar our purties, do ye uns hyar em, do ye?

She stops, and he does not want to open his eyes again, thinking,

She air still thar an in a bit she ull tell me whut I'm to do now.

From beyond the mountain comes a long, deep roll of thunder. He opens his eyes, raises his head and sniffs the air like an animal, his nostrils flaring to the smell of rain.

It are cumin, it are time to git up.

Pushing with his hands against his knees, he rises stiffly to his feet and almost falls he is so weak. He stands for a moment, gathering his strength and listening. In the beech grove and from beyond, where the laurel-hell begins on the first slope of the mountain, the whippoorwills are continuing to call over and over.

They uns are all thar with she an that other un now hits come dark.

He bends over, pulls the torch from the mound, holds it to the side above his shoulder, and starts to walk across the field toward the cabin. He has gone only a little way when he trips on a stone and almost falls. He stops to get his balance. Just beyond the edge of light, there is a faint rustling on the ground as though a breeze is moving through the dry corn stubble, but there is no breeze. The night air is still and heavy. He walks on, peering into the dark, trying to see if she is there; if she has come to see about him. To help him back. He holds the torch straight out and extends the light toward the sound. The rustling stops. The whippoorwills have stopped calling. He turns slowly in a circle, spreading the light all the way around. There is only dirt and weeds and stumps and stubble. He begins to walk again, and the rustling returns and continues before him as he walks out of the field into the beech grove and up the path to the door of the cabin, where the rustling stops.

The cabin is small and crudely built. Its clay-chinked logs are uneven, the floor is hard-packed dirt, there are no windows, and logs burn in the sandstone fireplace. The door is partially open. It hangs loosely on leather hinges. Through the opening, the fire's soft, yellowish light slants outward onto a hide-bottom chair that sits outside with its back against the log wall.

The tall man stands in the doorway but does not enter. Through the opening he sees the shapes of shadows moving on the wall and hears the rustling of corn-shucks in the tic that lies on the floor in the corner. He is so tired the bones in his body feel loose and barely able to hold him together.

He drops the torch onto the ground and slumps into the chair. The air smells of blood and wood smoke. He closes his eyes and it is all there again.

All of every day and every night returns as it was. He did not sleep and did not eat. He tried to help but nothing he did helped. No one had ever told him how it was to be done. Her words and moans went on and on and on until it came, still and quiet, and with it all of the blood. Then finally, it was over. And now he can barely hear her.

Holp me holp me.

I'm doin what I kin.

Mama are ye thar Mama?

She ain't hyar.

Mama holp me.

Shush now, ye uns'll tire ye sef.

Mama Mama Mama.

Shush now, I'm hyar.

He had taken her tiny hand and cupped it in both of his big, callused hands and held it as gently as if it was a baby bird. But it did not help.

They were alone. No one was there. No family, no granny woman, no neighbor. No one. They owned nothing; what little they had they had carried across the mountains on their backs and in their hands. They built the cabin but did not own it.

A man who had never set foot on this land, who did not even know what it looked like, a man whose name they would never know as he would never know theirs, owned the beech grove and the field and creek and the cove and all of the mountains around it; for miles and miles he owned every leaf and blade of grass and drop of water. He did not know they were here, and did not care, would never care, as long as they knew it was not theirs.

All the tall man had ever known was hardness. It had made him hard, except toward her. She was little more than a child, so small he could almost cover both of her hands when they were clasped together in one of his. The only thing she had ever wanted, she never had. When she had asked him for it, he had not looked at her, had not answered, had not even shaken his head.

She never asked again.

All those days and nights she had moaned and looked in his eyes for help. But she never prayed. Nor did he. They did not know how to pray. No one had taught them. They had never heard a prayer. They could not read or make letters. Their words to one another were few. Work was all they knew. It was all they had ever known, all they remembered or hoped for.

He opens his eyes and looks up at the sky.

The whippoorwills are silent.

Through the open door he hears her whisper,

Are ye thar?

I'm.

Ye hyar them purties?

I hyar.

I knowed ye'd be a lisnin.

I'm.

Can ye hyar him?

Wha?
He uns callin ye.
Ye bes git sum rest now.
I will if ye cum look.
I'll be thar.

The storm is almost here. Wind is starting to come down the mountain in gusts, shaking the leaves of the beeches, whirling dust upward.

The first drops of rain fall upon his face.

He will have to hurry. He stands, turns, and pushes the door all the way open.

THE SPIRIT

From 1817 to 1828, the John Bell family of Adams Station, Tennessee, was haunted by a spirit that eventually became known as the Bell Witch. There were nine Bell children. Among them, eleven year-old Betsy, was the one most tormented by the spirit. On a Sunday night, after a day of preaching, Reverend James Gunn, was invited to have supper with the Bells. When they finished eating, Reverend Gunn began to read scriptures; as he did the spirit spoke to Betsy who was standing at the window, hidden by curtains - watching, listening, speaking so softly her voice could not be heard.

Minister

Deuteronomy, chapter eighteen, verses ten through fourteen: There shall not be found among you anyone that maketh his son or his daughter pass through the fire, or that useth divination, or an observer of times, or an enchanter, or a witch, or a charmer, or consulter with familiar spirits, or a wizard, or a necromancer. For all that do these things are an abomination unto the Lord: and because of these abominations the Lord thy God doth drive them out from before thee. Thou shalt be perfect with the Lord thy God. First Samuel, twenty- eight, verses seven

through twenty five: Then said Saul unto his servants, Seek me a woman that hath a familiar spirit...

Spirit

O dear sweet, sweet girl, hear if you have ears to hear Old Sugarmouth's dark words rambling on and on in the night, seeking to strip sins away with King James, driving Deuteronomy in and out of wood, plaster, air, and flesh.

Betsy

Delicate and transparent as fine white skin, are lace curtains finely woven. Delicate finely spun webs covering windows black with night. Delectably, deliciously delicate, to touch, to taste, to wrap round face, arms, legs, to watch through, to rest a spider; delicate and soft, as white, soft hands immersed in whiteness. Watching others gathered together to discharge their curse. Minister, father, mother, brothers, sisters playing their child's game, searching for that to stay that which pulls them together in blood, in secret in word of God.

Minister

And the woman said unto Saul, I saw gods ascending out of the earth...

Spirit

Heed my words one by one, if a god comes on the earth your young bush will be burned with fire. For often he will make you pass through the fire in innocence, binding your long legs with wild grape vines, his face above you sweating and grunting. O sweet girl he who is continually coming up and out upon the earth shall be brought low before I go.

Betsy

Delectably watching him: tall, shrewd in his straight strength of body and mind. He listening intently without hearing the ineradicable rhythm of God's word, hearing beyond the tall windows open onto summer's hot darkness, beyond night winds whisperings, rumpling lace and skin, beyond the peeps of beasts and men.

Minister

Then Saul fell straightway all along on the earth, and was sore afraid, because of the words of Samuel: and there was no strength in him for he had eaten no bread all the day, nor all the night. And the woman came unto Saul, and saw that he was sore troubled, and said unto him, Behold, thine handmaid hath obeyed thy voice, and I put my life in my hand and have harkened unto thy words which thou spakest unto me...

Betsy

Riding above the winds and sounds of night he sits: strong arms folded, left hand hidden, right hand white in the light of the lamp, resting gently upon his sleeve, gently upon an arm heavy with strength and pleasure. Neither fearing, nor hating, nor loving, listening only to the amazement of a remembering, reviving in whispers over and over.

Spirit

Blood of my blood, bone of my bone, flesh of my flesh, know you not you are the temple of God, if any man defiles the temple of God him shall God destroy.

Minister

Leviticus, twenty-six through twenty-seven: And the soul that turneth after such as have familiar spirits, and after wizards, to go a whoring after them, I will even set my face against that soul, and will cut him off from among his people. Sanctify yourselves therefore, and be ye holy: for I am the Lord your God...

Betsy

In their circle they sit as for protection. Bound not by hands, nor by the minister's paralytic droning, nor by the six sides of simple, though skillfully woven, weatherboard that vertically and horizontally fixes their circle as a cross into the rich, red land; nor even by their common source of earth and blood, but by the known and unknown knowledge of their secrets. Larger than shadows he sits. Listening. A conqueror conquered in his own strength; he who conquered forest and land and family. Sitting. His face turned half away.

Minister

And if a man lie with a beast, he shall surely be put to death: and ye shall slay the beast. And if a woman approach unto any beast, and lie down thereto, thou shall kill the woman, and the beast: they shall surely be put to death; their blood shall be upon them...

Spirit

You that have ears to hear, let them hear: the desolation of houses where the beasts of the forests lie and owls dwell and satyrs dance; hear the wild beasts of the air cry in their desolation and dragons in their pleasant palaces. Your time is near at hand. Your days shall not be prolonged.

Betsy

Shades of red and black and white flicker and fade. The lace draws tighter round. Dead still they sit. Watching. Mouths open. Wondering at the milk and honey under their tongues.

Spirit

O dear sweet girl, hear rather the genesis and revelations that come flickering from my mouth; a serpent's tongue testing the dark for the hidden one who comes from the forest running, leaping, shedding his skin of sin, drunk in his tremendous whiteness; a new child of God freshly risen from the Red River, running, leaping like a rutting deer. My testing tongue tells he comes grunting in glory. He comes and goes in the dark. His shadow swirls and turns black.

Betsy

Will he not turn and see through the lace, a face faced by enemies smiling on suffering and winking their eyes, that hate? Yes! They open their mouths wide and say, our eyes have seen through the delicate and transparent lace and forest. Nothing has been hidden from those who watch in secret the bright red spot of light rising in darkness. Will he set his face forever away? Turn now and see through the tears and sweat that leave their drippings on cheek and breast. Sorrows and shouts have been heard and not forgotten. Let them not smile. Let them rather shout in joy for the joy given!

Spirit

The sounds of our beloved! He comes leaping over mountains, dancing upon hills. Flowers appear before him, singing birds are all around, the turtle's voice is heard in the land and our vines have tender grapes. He is a buck feeding upon lilies and I am the Lily of the Valley. The earth trembles and shakes.

Betsy

The breeze stops. The single, coal-oil lamp, clean and bright, mingles its scents with others secretly hanging in the still and heavy air and gives life to shadows joining together without definition or darkness.

Spirit

Behold! The hidden one comes leaping and dancing hand in hand with all things created in the beginning. He comes. He comes. leaping and dancing upon the earth. The earth heaves and opens. Behold! He comes! He comes!

Betsy

Bound round and round with lace - squealing and panting for joy!

Minister

A man also or a woman that hath a familiar spirit, or that is a wizard, shall surely be put to death: they shall stone them with stones: their blood shall be upon them...

Betsy

To and fro, to and fro, to and fro, rocking in rhythm to the word of the Lord.

Spirit

O sweet, sweet love, dip now your hand into the Red River. Know you the hidden one comes for burial in water, love and blood. Know you his sacrifice, is your salvation. Know you God's will. Rise and sacrifice an offering unto God, young, white, delicate as lace.

Betsy

Listening now to his eternal listening. With him, as one, listening to whisperings rending round all in all. Listening to lace and skin tearing away layer by layer. Listening until at last all is stripped bare and the hidden one rises fresh and white – Listen! - Aha now they all listen and watch. And now all their mouths are open. Behold! Behold! Behold! He turns! He rises! He comes looking full upon a sweet, sweet, white face clean of lace.

Spirit

Hear now you that have ears to hear! Hear now the leaping and the dancing! Hear now the genesis and the exodus! Hear now, the hidden one, coming and going in the dark!

Minister

Exodus twenty-two, verse eighteen: Thou shalt not suffer a witch to live.

LAFE

Lafayette Washington Pearson
1860 - 1878

Lafe

Once't, when I wus born, I wus two people, Angel an Lafe together, all at tha same time, an somehow or other Angel weren't right, she could nair walk, nair talk, nair care fer herself, but I loved her dearly anyways since she wus me; so I went up in tha barn loft an prayed ta God ta make her right, an I cuts my arms an bled all over ta shed blood fer her, an I ask im that made us ta make us over agin, but He didn't do nuthin, we jus stayed like we wus; so's I became jes Lafe by myself, an I stays away in tha woods from Angel an Nanny an tha other'ns, much as I could; but all that happened a long while later, a long while after tha giant came on me on his big black horse outta tha trees; an when I think on hit, I still hyair his voice an smell im an see im killin my dog, Queenie, an then killin Daddy an Brother.

Nanny

Fer a long bit hit wair a mystery ta me, why neither of tha twins wair made right; they'uns jes weren't natural, they wair not hardly like human beins from tha first when they'uns come outa me, cept maybe Lafe he'uns seemed normal until what happened ta im, but you'uns could see Angel weren't. I studied on hit fer a long while an then I prayed on hit fer a long while an then, one day, hit come ta me, that hit wair a punishment brought down on me fer my ways with tha Garner boys, a long way back when I wus only a youngun an had nairy a bit of sense. But I guess from tha Lord's way uv lookin at hit I wus sinnin an had ta pay tha price. But hit don't seem right that Angel an Lafe had ta suffer fer my sins; tha Lord should uv jes done sumpin ta me an be done with hit but, no, them pore thangs, specially Lafe, lived most in misery; but thair's somethin good an different inside Angel that sumtimes I think's maybe like a real angel. I seed hit, fer she'uns wus always happy, even tho she can't tell hit ta us in words. Oh dair God, fergive me fer bringin tha sufferin on her.

Jeremiah

The first time I saw him he was coming straight toward me down a long field through the first soft-gray light of ev'nin. He looked like a young Viking: slender and fair with long blonde hair spread across his shoulders, his face as pretty as a girl's with full lips and long eyelashes; his movements smooth as water; his eyes pale, unblinking, cold and hard, the eyes of a killer. He wore patched dove-gray pants, no shirt and an unbuttoned, threadbare blue cavalry jacket and no shoes. In the crook of his right arm was a double-barrel shotgun, stuck in his pants was a Colt pistol and a long skinning knife was sheathed in a scabbard attached to a wide leather belt around his waist. He had two large brindle hounds with him, one on each side. He was fourteen.

Lafe

I wus four, when hit all happened. I still see hit an hyair hit...Queenie smelt em first. She set ta barkin, an runnin back an forth right side me in tha wagon, an when she seed all em horsemen a comin outa tha woods, she went ta growlin. They'uns so quiet at first, Daddy an Brother didn't see or hyair em, fer they're choppin on tha farwood but then tha horsemen rode up all round us an they stopped choppin. One of em was a giant. He wus on a big black horse an he come right up side tha wagon, right next ta me an I commenced ta shiverin. He look so much like a big bear ridin on a horse; I could barely see his eyes when they'uns looked down at me through all that hair an beard coverin his face over. He skeered me so I pretended ta be daid an hoped he'd think so too, an go away. But he nairy went. He reached down an grabbed a hold uv me an hitched me up an spread-legged me round his neck so's I's facin toward Daddy an Brother. All tha other horsemen had gotten down off their horses an were standin all round em; an when I see'd my Daddy I didn't call ta im or cry cause I wus daid.

Nairy a one hep me, not even God. Maybe He wus daid too, fer thair come a time way later on, when I knowed He'd died too. Tha giant's hair stank an got grease on me, an I wus hurtin twixt my legs where I'd been pull't down hard. Two men, jes alikes, were beatin on Daddy an Brother while tha other'uns held em; then they started a cutting on em an Daddy was cussin an Brother nastied hisself. Queenie jumped from tha wagon through tha air an grabbed hold of tha giant's arm an bit im an he took hold of her an twisted her head an pitched her ta tha ground, an she nair moved agin. An I member tha mule's eyes gettin all big but thair bodies nair moved or made a sound; they'uns pretendin they'uns daid too. Then tha giant, he lifted me round in front of im an kiss me full on tha mouth an set me easy back in tha wagon an shouted at tha look alikes ta get thair hair an finish hit all up. Though my eyes be daid they seen Daddy an Brother's skin an hair cut off thair heads an tha jest alikes tied tha hair ta tha reins uv tha giant's horse an they'uns put ropes round Daddy an Brother's necks an haul'd em way high up in a tree, then they'uns all rode off. But I jes stayed daid fer apiece til Nanny an tha girls come. An when they seed hit all thair eyes got scairt lookin at what wair up in tha tree but I weren't scairt cause I wus daid an I hain't aire been scairt agin.

Lillie Jane

Lafe was killed when I had just turned four so I barely remember him. What little I do remember is mostly sad and unpleasant; the fact be known, he sometimes scared me. At night, when my sisters and I were in bed, we could hear him up in the loft talking to himself and making sounds that were more like a wild animal than a human. One time, I heard him in the kitchen with Angel—they were alone—he was talking to her like they were having a conversation. He'd make moaning sounds just like she did, as though she was talking back to him. It made me run and hide. He was different than anyone I had ever known, different more than even Angel. There were two things that "marked him" as Nanny used to say about terrible happenings and what they could do to children: The first must have been a horror, for he was only four when he saw Daddy and Brother being killed right in front of him; then they were scalped; my Lord, that's beyond my imagining. The second was Angel's deformity. Nanny told me how he tried to get God to make her right. He cut his arms until they were covered in blood. When Angel was not changed into a perfect girl, Lafe turned his back on God and even on us. He began staying to himself, sleeping for days out in the woods, hunting and killing animals, coming to the house for only a day or so and then he was gone again.

Jeremiah

Lafe has never left me. After all these years, there are times I conjure him up in my mind and see him standing in the doorway as clearly as I see my hand writing, his beautiful face, his pale eyes fixed on mine, his dogs by his side. I hear his voice demanding, '*Now, by God, tell me why yair hyair?*' For a moment I tense up, as I did long ago, then he is gone.

How could this strange boy have been my wife's brother? It was as if he and Lillie Jane came from different parents. He was fair, somber, easy to anger, with the language of the mountains; she was dark, smiling, filled with laughter and color whose speech is that of one who is well educated, which she is.

When I was with Lafe I was careful with my words and movements. He could be abrupt and would flare up if anyone, even his mother, opposed him. Yet with all of this, I was awed by his independence, his brilliance in the wild and his harsh honesty. The more we were together, the more I wanted to be like him.

When we were in the woods, if he sensed the presence of an animal or a human, he would throw up his arm for me to stop. Except for the flaring of his nostrils he would stand still as a stone; his whole being would be fixed on whatever he saw or heard or felt was nearby. His eyes darted back and forth; he sniffed the air like an animal; the tip of his tongue would flick out and twitch as he tasted the air. If it had been possible, his ears would have twisted and turned like a deer's.

Though I know it is foolish, it has gone through my mind that he wasn't quite human; yet I never thought he was insane or possessed. The old woman, Maw-ree, who lived in a cave on the side of the mountain and who some called a witch, was with me when I first saw Lafe coming up the field. She said, '*Dat un comin der be a debil.*' No, that is not right; she was wrong, for though he was different than anyone I've ever known, Lafe was not a devil. Within him I could see the little boy, loving his father and brother who were slaughtered before his eyes; and I could see the brother whose heart was broken as he heard his sister, twisted in her crib, moaning over and over. How can such terror and sadness ever be known by anyone of us?

Nanny

After he seen Nathaniel an James kilt by John Gaunt an his trash, Lafe turned different an thair weren't a bit of joy left in im. An after he cut hisself all up fer Angel an hit nairy changed her, that's when tha demon got in im an from then on he acted like he ain't got no more carin fer anyone. He quit lookin at Angel, an, if we'uns go ta tech im, he'd pull away. He even made a fist at me onct an had a look in his eye like he'd hit me if I laid a hand on im. He'd usually jest grunt or look away if ya said airy a thang to im. His eyes'd git all dead lookin an, at night, when he wus in tha loft, he'd laugh an holler an shout blackguards an thair's times he'd growl an his voice'd go deep inside im like he wus someone else.

All those last yairs, fore he wus kilt, he'd hardly hit a lick ta hep us with tha stock or crops. Tha biggest part uv his time wus spent with his dogs an guns back in tha woods an on tha mountin. When he'd kill somethin he bloodied his face an put tha meat on tha table an ud start actin out how he'd kilt hit an cut hit's throat; an he'd git ta makin tha gun sounds an tha dyin sounds. His eyes'd be all big an shiny til he stopped then they'd go daid agin, an he'd go up ta tha loft an fall asleep. Lookin back on hit all, hit aire a great sadness—fer he wair my baby boy...my baby boy.

Lafe

Tha Cove's full uv spirits, specially in tha cave or mongst tha beeches whair tha Injuns worshiped. Tha spirits nairy trouble me fer I leave em offerins on tha oak tree atop tha cliff above tha Sink.

Jeremiah

"Shit, yer still a kid an don't know nairy bout killin but by God I'll turn ya inta a killer. We'll kill that sumbitch Sheriff an tha otherns." That's what Lafe promised me. The next morning he took me into the woods above the Sink to a tree where he had hung carcasses, skulls, skins of animals and feathers of birds. While I watched, he circled the tree chanting over and over, "Tutsihusi, Tutsihusi, Tutsihusi," a Cherokee word that meant, "Die...die...die."

I killed my first deer, a doe, a week later. As we knelt beside her Lafe put both of his hands on her body, closed his eyes and said something that sounded like another language then pulled his knife from its scabbard, cut her throat and let the blood flow over his hands. He lifted them, turned to me and rubbed the blood over my face and in my hair. "Now, ye be baptized in tha name of tha one who loves killers." With that, he sliced her stomach open, reached inside, cut her heart out and handed it to me. "Eat hit! Eat ever speck uv hit!"

Three years later, when I was fourteen and he eighteen, we killed a giant she-bear, the last bear killed in Lost Cove. She killed two of our dogs and nearly killed Lafe. When he shot her, she charged and fell on him. I thought he was dead. Just as she was about to bite him I shot her in the eye and finished her. It was quiet for a minute, then I heard laughter and Lafe rolled from under her, covered in blood, "Jeremiah, yer ready. Hits time fer us ta kill that sumbitch Sheriff an em other sumbitches!"

Lafe

God let Angel die but I didn't cause I kept her alive all inside me whair we'uns talk all tha time, most at night, an she'uns ull tell me she loves me an I tell her I love her. But sometimes, we'uns git ta arguing, specially bout me likin ta kill things, but I tells her I can't hep hit fer hit takes some uv tha hurt in me away fer a bit. Fer I still see Daddy an Brother daid up in em trees all tha time, an I git so scairt hit drives me ta want ta kill tha giant an his'uns. So I tlls Angel ta stop fussin at me cause I got tag it ready fer killin em. So I keep on killin wild things an Angel keeps on fussin though I know she still loves me cause I can see hit in her face an she can still see hit in mine.

Lillie Jane

On December 22, 1878, my brother, Lafayette Washington Pearson, and Jeremiah Vann killed Sheriff John Gaunt, his sister Lucy Taggert and her sons, Sam and Hubert Taggert, on the road between Sewanee and Sherwood; Lafe was killed by John Gaunt. We buried him beside Daddy and Brother in the Pearson cemetery in Lost Cove the next day.

Nanny

Losin yair babies might nigh kills ya; hit nair leaves ya. Tha hurtin's waitin thair ever mornin right side yair bed.

RUNES

Rune *(roon)*

Noun 1. Any of the letters of the earliest Germanic alphabet, used esp. by the Scandinavians and Anglo Saxons from around the 3rd cent. AD, and formed by modifying Roman or Greek characters to facilitate carving on wood or stone: a similar character or mark believed to have some magical power of significance. Also a character of a non-Germanic or esp. ancient alphabet. 2. An incantation, a charm esp. one denoted by magic or cryptic signs; a magical word.

Oxford English Dictionary

300.7 – Body Dysmorphic Disorder

The essential feature of Body Dysmorphic Disorder is a preoccupation with a defect in appearance. The defect is either imagined, or, if a slight physical anomaly is present, the individual's concern is markedly excessive... Most individuals experience marked distress over their supposed deformity, often describing their preoccupations as "intensely painful," or " devastating." As a result, they often spend hours a day thinking about their "defect," to the point where their thoughts may dominate their lives. Significant impairment in many areas of functioning generally occurs. Feelings of self-consciousness about their "defect" may lead to avoidance of work or public situations.

Desk Reference to The Diagnostic Criteria From DSM-IV

I am consumed by despair and hate.

The tip of my right forefinger touches my tongue then slowly skims across my face. In the bathroom mirror I watch it trace the carvings in my flesh, the crumbling eyelids and lips, the gray skin, the thinning hair and the sockets deepening into darkness. I see the mortification and necrotizing from the bacteria feeding within.

My wife argues with me to the point I want to choke her. She says that these are just the lines and liver spots and wastings of old age. She begs for me to stop constantly staring into mirrors and feeling my face. Her fussing and begging make me hate her more than I already do. Damn it to hell, I am contaminated by some disease or curse her stupid doctor's tests are incapable of detecting. I'd kill her before ever returning to see him. I no longer leave the house.

Nothing slows its progress: the salves, heat lamps, the Epsom soakings and prayers might as well be piss. Every food preached to be good for skin is useless: salmon, eggs, blueberries, spinach, gallons of orange juice and those pathetic avocados pass through my body and the decay continues. They are no better than my own defecation. How could they remove the poison that entered me in my mother's blood and milk.

My scars are the runes Mother carved into my soul, if I it exists. She was incapable of mothering. Oh yes, she fed me and kept my clothes clean but she never kissed me or hugged me, never said, "I love you." The only time she ever used the word "love" was when she was speaking of God. How then was I conceived by a woman barren of any sexual passion except for the lover who lived in her mind? Did my father rape her? Or am I a child of an immaculate conception from the One she professed to love above all?

The Bible was the air that filled our house. It was my teacher, the principal of my schooling. Its word was the whip across my hands and back.

Only fear of hell stopped me from killing her. I should have done it when I first thought of it when I was six. She had whipped me with a telephone cord until I bled because I couldn't name all the books in the Old Testament. Since I could not, God should have killed her for me. He should have protected me. But He did not. Surely He did not create me to suffer as I have. Or did He? How could I be the way I am if not by His wish? Did He want a monster?

I entered hell from my mother's womb. I have read and reread His words. I prayed His prayers. Yet torment has never left me. Awake or asleep I see and smell the devastation, the deeply cut characters of damnation in my face and blood and brain.

Just a fingernail length beneath my right eye is a tiny crack shaped like a fallen cross leaning sideways in the earth. It can only be seen with a magnifying glass that exposes the truth hidden beneath cryptic disguises. My flesh is filled with fallen crosses. I've tried to show them to my wife, but she only turns her back, shrugs and says she has them all over her body. When she says such things I have a quick flash of my mother's face. More and more they are the same.

I am not sure I ever loved her, my wife that is. I may not have been able to. We no longer sleep together. I cannot bear the thought of her lying beside me, smelling the stench that oozes from my pores at night. I can barely stand it myself. If she were to smell it, it would only be another reason to berate me. Every morning, I shower and spray deodorant over my entire body.

Thank God we have no children to perpetuate eternal punishment to their descendants. I thank Him for nothing else.

Tonight, before I fall asleep, my last thought will be of killing her.

BENEATH THE STAIRS

Journal of Evan Williams
Dyserth Plantation
Haywood County, Tennessee
December 25, 1990

Forgive
Us forgive
Us your death that myselves the believers
May hold it in great flood
Till the blood shall spurt,
And the dust shall sing like a bird
As the grains blow, as your death grows, through our heart

Dylan Thomas

When I was nine, Branwen and I found our mother hanging beneath the stairs.

We are a large and proud family; here for long generations, mixing our Welsh and English and Irish and Cherokee bloods into the bones of our faces, our colors, the sizes and shapes of our bodies. The richness of our blood and our land has carried us upward as the depth of the fertile Delta slopes towards us.

"Senator Father," United States Senator William Williams, Master of Dyserth, my father, was in Washington D.C. most of World War II. He came home only to campaign at election time and to vote, and for two days in the spring and fall to meet with his overseers. He came once for Christmas in 1942 but, on December 25 and 26, 1945, he was not there; he was in Washington.

I am his only son. I was nine years old that Christmas of 1945, forty-five years ago. My sister, Branwen, was eight. Other than the Negro pickaninnys and the overseer's brats, we were the only children for miles in every direction. We were never with clean white children until we were sent away.

Our cotton, corn, and timber stretch outward over seventeen thousand acres of fat, gently rolling land separated into five plantation sections. Through it, like a water moccasin, twists the muddy Hatchie River. The cotton and corn are sold in Memphis, an hour's drive away. Until his death, Senator Father was a member of the board of the Memphis Cotton Exchange. Now, I am its chairman.

Shiny-black African slaves created our fields from swamp and forest. We owned five hundred of them. Now, fewer than four hundred Negro tenants plow and plant, weed, pick, gin, and bale the white gold that rises from the black soil. Their intensity of color has softened as the generations have passed, from tawny, to hazel, until now you see fewer and fewer of the old shiny, jet-blacks. There are more Negroes than whites in Haywood, and they scheme to wrest control from me. They have not. With few exceptions, the whites remain, as always, "trash," but still they follow me. Now, I, master of Dyserth, observe these changes and constancies of time, and note them in my journal.

*****

Lead bought our land and slaves. Who we are began with my great grandfather, Dafydd Williams', lead mine in Denbighshire, Wales. He sold it in 1822. With its proceeds he booked passage on a clipper to New Orleans. From there, he came up the Mississippi and overland to Haywood. He named his nine hundred acres Dyserth, after his home village. With him he brought seven slaves, his wife, and their only child, my grandfather, Huw Williams.

Six years before the war, Dafydd died from yellow fever contracted while buying slaves in Memphis. He left five thousand acres, one-hundred and fifty slaves, two gins, a ferry, mill, hundreds of cattle, horses and oxen and a two story, six room brick house, with white pillared porches, front and rear.

Like Abraham, my grandfather, the inheritor of Dyserth, increased our land and wealth. He built the "Big House," the largest and grandest house in West Tennessee. Six great Doric columns span the front portico and verandah. Above the hipped roof rises a cupola, windowed on every side; from there, as far as you can see is Williams' land. The house's walls are four spans of red brick made from our own earth. It stands like a Greek temple on a slight rise, three-quarters of a mile from the river. To its rear, a long English Boxwood garden and walk lead to an octagonal observatory built for parties never held. A little ways beyond is our cemetery, surrounded by an iron fence.

Our fields are our power in Haywood County. From them comes our control of Tennessee and some of Washington. My father was its king. He created state legislators and governors one after another; despising them all along with his constituents. He once told me, "Our family rules over the rabble of the earth." From a distance you would have thought him an impeccably dressed boy, he was so small. But standing before him, looking into his emotionless black eyes, you saw one you would not oppose. The face in the mirror when he shaved was God's.

*****

An old schoolmate of Mother's told me that even as a young girl she was "delicate," a word long past, a word once used for genteel ladies given to melancholy. Oh my God, she was beautiful: tall, willowy-slender, with slow languid movements. Her face ethereal as Raphael's *Mary*! The only daughter of the wealthy Episcopal Bishop of Memphis, she was the Queen of the Cotton Carnival in 1931, her father's riches reaped from his father's slave market in New Orleans. I believed she was God's final perfection. More than anything in my childhood, I wanted her love. Everyone called her "Darlin."

My father met her the year she was crowned at the Carnival. Mother was seventeen, he twenty-seven. Two months later they married, and ten months after that I was born. The year after came Branwen, my precocious sister. The next year a boy was born dead and seven months later she miscarried. She almost died. The doctor said she would die if she were pregnant again. From that time on she rarely left the house, except to attend Holy Day services at Zion Episcopal Church in Brownsville. Once a month, the priest came to Dyserth for lunch with Mother, to deliver a blessing on our family and on our land. Later, when I was grown, I wondered if his deliverance was a curse.

*****

Except for dear old Aunt Rit - the daughter of two of our slaves - who oversaw our house servants and those who kept the yards and gardens - and, an ignorant, insipid tutor who came twice a week, Branwen and me were left mostly to ourselves to grow up. Within this emptiness of neglect, we created our own world and lived in it most of every day and in all of our dreams.

We filled our days with rhymes from *The Real Mother Goose.* Its words were so instilled in our hearts, that we came to believe we had written them, most especially those that spoke of death.

The great hallway was our kingdom. On the hottest of summer days, air moves through its large doorways when they are open at both ends. Ten strides in from the front door rises the grand elliptical stairway. Not a home - not even in Memphis - has such a magnificent stairway. Gleaming mahogany, it floats in air as it curves upward, its steps wide enough for four people to walk side-by-side. As Branwen and I sat beneath them our imaginations became reality and the words of Mother Goose told us who we were, and what we were to do.

The Death And Burial Of Poor Cock Robin was our favorite. Branwen began the chant and I followed,

Branwen: "Who killed Cock Robin"
Me: "I", said the sparrow,
"With my little bow and arrow,
"I killed Cock Robin."

Branwen: "Who saw him die?"
Me: "I", said the fly,
"With my little eye,
"I saw him die."

Branwen: "Who caught his blood?"
Me: "I", said the fish,
"With my little dish,
"I caught his blood."

Branwen, "Who'll make his shroud?"
Me: "I", said the beetle,
"With my thread and needle,
"I'll make his shroud."

Branwen: "Who'll dig his grave?"
Me: "I", said the owl,
"With my spade and trowel,
"I'll dig the grave."

So, we passed our long days during the summer of '45. At first we pretended. Then, we began to kill.

Instead of a robin I killed a Rhode Island Red rooster with my bow and arrow. After I pulled the arrow out, Branwen made a coffin from a doll box. We put the coffin into the grave we had dug in the cemetery. We held hands and, with our eyes closed, we chanted together,

"Who'll carry the coffin?
"I", said the kite,
"If it's not in the night,
"I'll carry the coffin."

"Who'll toll the bell?
"I," said the bull,
"Because I can pull,
"I'll toll the bell."

With that, she rang the small bell Mother used to call the servants.

"All the birds of the air
"Fell sighing and sobbing,
"When they heard the bell toll
"For poor Cock Robin."

For a moment we acted sad, and Branwen actually cried. It was quiet. Then Branwen began to laugh and I laughed. It was wonderful!

*****

My God, Branwen was beautiful, a mirror of Mother. She dressed in black and swished her skirts, like mother, when she talked.

Her eyes were fox eyes: vixen's, quick, watching, seeing everything; a hunting brilliance, shrewdness that looked into me, through me, commanded me, as though I was naked. I did not know the word then but there were times I believed she was preternatural. When she was absorbed in a book (at age five she began taking books from our father's library), or practicing her writing or drawing, I would stare at her for long moments, until finally, she raised her eyes – with the smile she had for me at night – and would motion for me to come close to her, close up against her and, when we were touching, she would read to me or tell me the story of her drawing.

We slept together, Branwen and me. At night, as soon as Aunt Rit heard our prayers, tucked us in, turned out the light, and left the room, Branwen's feet hit the floor and she came to me under the covers, pulling herself against me, into our curved bodies.

Even after we were sent far away, to boarding schools, we were together again at Dyserth in the summer and Christmas. My God, how I loved seeing her, feeling her body as we hugged, her lips as we kissed.

Oh yes, Branwen, I would have married you.

I dream of you. Of us touching. Even now, married, with children, my dreams come with erections and more. Oh yes, if you had not been my sister, I would have married you. Oh, my Branwen, you are always within me.

*****

Killing and burying Cock Robin was so much fun we acted it out, over and over, for days. We laid flowers on the grave and chanted our lines. A week later, we were bored.

"I'm tired of doing Cock Robin," I said.

"What do you want to do next?" Branwen asked.

"How about Humpty Dumpty?"

She squnched her nose up, "Stinkweed. That's just an egg."

"Well." And we thought.

"I know what...let's do Ladybird."

And we did.

> "Ladybird, ladybird, fly away home!
> "Your house is on fire, your children all gone,
> "All but one, and her name is Ann,
> "And she crept under the pudding pan."

I struck a match to a piece of paper and held the flame beneath a nest in a lilac bush in the cemetery.

Brenwan slipped a sewing thimble over the head of the smallest of the four chirping chicks. It was over in a moment. 'Ann' did not survive.

*****

As we would not have survived without Aunt Rit's hugs and kisses.

"You babies come ova heah an give ol Aunt Rit a big ol hug an I'll tell you a story." And she would pull us to her and begin,

"My great-granddaddy be Gumpa Keeby; he wus bawn across tha big watah an wus always tellin us bout his dreams uv Africa an how he'd see big ol long-neckt animals an ones with hawns an big teeth an claws an he'd get ta makin roarin sounds an hissin an scare us might nigh ta death an we'd scream an run an then he jus laugh an laugh. Ya'll think ol Aunt Rit's black, my granddaddy wus tha blackest human bein God evah made." And all the while she talked she was smiling down on us like sunshine. Finally, she'd let go of us and, with a stern smile, say, "You chullin get on now an let ol Aunt Rit git goin cause I knows someuns slackin off their doins."

How could we have stayed alive without the warmth and love of this good woman wrapped around us? We were starved for love and she was our air and food and life. Still, I hear her words, smell the smell of her King

Leo Peppermint, feel her heavy breasts and arms pressing against my face; I taste her turnip greens, white beans, fried chicken, and peach pie. Even now, in my guilt, she brings me some comfort.

But, for Branwen and me, her love was not enough to stop us. So we continued to kill.

******

All with the direction of our rhymes we next killed a crow and a duck and cut off the tails of three baby blind mice with one of Aunt Rit's carving knives.

Then we were ready for "Precious Baby."

Mother's fat, stupid, calico cat had green eyes. Mother loved her more than Branwen and me. For long periods of every day that thing laid in the bed beside Mother with its eyes closed. If not there, then it lay in its loaf of bread position, sunning itself, on the windowsill in the front parlor. We hated that cat for every stroke and pat she received from Mother. We decided to kill her.

"Which rhyme shall we use?" asked Branwen.

"I'm thinking."

"I know!"

"What?"

"Ding, Dong, Bell,
"Pussy's in the well!
"Who put her in?
"Little Tommy Lin."

"Oh gosh, no, not that one 'cause Johnny Stout saves her…Here it is…Here's the one."

"Hush-a-bye, baby, on the tree top!
"When the wind blows the cradle will rock;
"When the bough breaks the cradle will fall;
"Down will come baby, bough, cradle and all."

"Yes! Yes!"

And that's what we did.

While Mother was gone to Zion for Christmas Holy Day,

We put Precious Baby in a doll cradle and carried her up to the cupola.

Her eyelids barely lifted once, then twice, then closed.

I opened the front window and stepped out onto the roof.

Branwen handed the cradle out to me.

Slowly, I eased down the roof above the front portico.

A foot from the edge, I stopped and looked back at Branwen.

She smiled and whispered, "Down will come baby, bough, cradle and all."

And I pitched the cradle over the edge to the stones below.

The next day, we found Mother hanging beneath the stairs.

Did we do it?

If so, forgive us Lord!

I see her face clearly after all these years.

Most especially on Holy Days.

Branwen was twenty-one when she cut her wrists and died.

I will end with the following which I came on yesterday while reading Thornton Wilder's, *The Bridge of San Luis Rey*. And with this sentence all that summer and winter of 1945 came back as though it was now:

> *Some say we shall never know and that to the Gods we are like flies that the boys kill on a summer day, and some say, on the contrary, that the very sparrows do not lose a feather that has not been brushed away by the finger of God.*

Were Mother and Senator Father and Branwen and I only flies, or feathers, brushed away by the finger of God?

WOLF SKIN

How could I have loved my mother so much after all she did? But I did love her more than anyone or anything in my life. I worshipped her, and still do, even though I now wonder if she was my mother—if I am from her egg or blood.

******

On the library wall, behind the desk where I am writing, hangs a Russian, she-wolf skin; six feet, nine inches long. It is beautiful. When she was killed she weighed 190 pounds.

The overall color is tawny or rufous gray. The head, back to the neck, shoulders, loins, and hindquarters are blackish with yellow tints. There is a very dense brown under fur intermixed with white and black hairs. The thighs and outer the legs are reddish yellow. The tail is dark brown above and lighter below and tipped with black. The mask is a mix of white and dark brown covered with short velvety fur with black whiskers. It glows, as though alive.

******

A few days from now I will be eighty. I have never married. Have no children. No brother or sister. My few cousins are near death; long ago they stopped talking to me. I practiced psychiatry for twenty years then, founded an investment company, which made me wealthy. But in recent years my wealth has been greatly reduced by the plunge in oil prices and the stock market. Wealth once gave me great satisfaction. No more. My fortune, which exceeded $300,000,000, has been cut to far less than a third of that; the stupidity of my financial advisers and bankers have brought this about. Their names and home addresses are on a list in the top drawer of my desk.

There are times, when the moon is full I only see darkness in myself. As I near the end of my life I have an overpowering need to reveal the darkness and secrets I've never told anyone, not even my analyst. They are obsessions filling my dreams, nightmares returning over and over, of demons and fantasies, beliefs and disbeliefs and lusts and obsessions that often control me at night, things that I hope this telling will cast out. If not, Freud was a "Fool" and psychoanalysis is no more than babble.

How strange I use the word "demons" for I do not believe in them as I do not believe in a god or devil. After I die there will be no soul left behind to mark my passing, only my journal, which will be published by my attorney. It will tell of the horror that has been within me since I was a boy, horror that has prevented me from ever loving another—except for my mother. I've tried to control it with mental tricks and the many pills I eat. They have all failed, even foolish incantations and fasts have not removed the pain and demons tearing and howling in me. You may understand why when you have read my story.

******

My mother had a dog named "Ulf."

But...I'm getting ahead of myself.

Let me start again...start before I was born...start with my parents.

This is what my mother told me, but like many things she said it may not be true: "Our people were little more than serfs for generations. We lived and died on the lands of the Duke of Bavaria whose family had owned tens of thousands of sections stretching for miles across the valleys and mountains. Reichsburg, his castle, stood at the top of one of the Utersberg Mountains that surrounded the small town of Berchtesgaden. Your father was the Duke's head Gamekeeper. I was a healer. You were born in 1936. You were our only child."

I see her, the night of my seventh birthday, crushing herbs into a clay bowl, rubbing the pulp into the wolf skin. She suddenly looked up and said, "You are old enough now to hear how your father died; he was killed by a wolf. He had killed hundreds of them and never been hurt, not even scratched, but in the winter of 1938, two years after you were born, he was killed by a huge Russian she-wolf." She put her hands on the skin. "This is hers; I have kept it is as fresh as when she was killed." She leaned her face into it and did not speak again.

The next night she continued, "Your father had gone into the mountains, to 'The High Forest,' to hunt a wolf that was killing the Duke's cattle. Neither he, nor his three wolfhounds, returned." She suddenly paused and said something strange, "I am a Jew. Your father wasn't. I hated Hitler and the Nazis. We were...we are Jews...Hitler was a wolf. The Germans followed him like sheep. The Nazis killed most of my aunts and uncles and cousins. They would have killed us if we hadn't gotten away." I did not understand who Hitler and the Nazis were.

She continued, "The party searching for your father followed the trail through the snow into early afternoon. The snow had stopped. The tracks led into the forest. Ahead, they heard loud crackling and squawking of crows coming through the trees. As they came into a small glade the air was filled with crows flaring up from a slaughter pen of blood.

"The wolf was feeding on your father. They shot her nine times.

"They brought your father's body back and the skin of the wolf that had killed him. They gave the skin to me. Two days later, we buried your father in the section of the Duke's cemetery where his favorite gamekeepers were buried.

"That night I began to scrape and clean the skin. Then when I finished, I salted it and hung it on the side of our house to cure. When it was ready I took it down and began to rub pulp from plants and herbs and animal grease into it—to keep it alive. When it was ready I took the money I had saved and hidden in the cellar and fled with you to Switzerland, then to the United States, then to the South where land was cheap."

******

Our house was a rough-framed, wood-shingled cabin in the middle of the mountains, a few miles south of Sewanee, Tennessee. It sat on the side of a steep ravine that sloped to Crow Creek, which flowed from Buggytop Cave to the village of Sherwood and beyond. Covered in forest, the mountains around us were like a wall across the southern border of the state.

The people were poor, hard working, mostly good, decent people. All but a few accepted my mother because she could heal them and bring their babies into the world alive—but a few, like the Dorton twins, hated us as some of our ways were different and our speech strange to their ears—they called us "Kraut Jews" and said we should be run out of the mountains since we were "likely Hitler spies." Others called her the "Witch of Lost Cove" and swore that when the cove flooded they had seen her float across it in an eggshell.

Every night she rubbed her special oils into the skin. The hair glistened as though alive and when she stroked the fur against her face and touched it to her lips she whispered words I had never heard.

******

On September 28, 1939, eight days before my third birthday, the night was filled with moonlight. Objects were as clear as the black ink on this white paper I am writing my life upon. I had not been in bed long. The light from the moon coming through the single window in the loft where I slept was so bright I could not fall asleep.

Looking down from the window I saw who I thought was my mother come from the shadows of the house on all fours. She was completely covered by what seemed to be the wolf skin.

******

The next day, the Dorton twins, Sandy Joe and West Wild, were found lying face up beside their still at the north end of Lost Cove. Their faces were twisted in horror, their throats torn out. There was no evidence of who had killed them, no shoe or boot-prints, nothing—except for the paw prints of what the Sheriff, in the *Winchester Home Journal,* called "the gosh awfulest, biggest paw prints of a dog, or what ever it was, I'd ever seen in all my years. Two of em were in blood smack-dab on Sandy Joe's chest. Whatever that thing was it must have been almost as big as a yearlin calf. I tell you one thing, we'd better get it fore it gets someone else. I'm lookin for volunteers to bring their rifles an sharpest nosed hounds an meet me in front of the Sewanee Chapel this Saturday at 9:00 AM to run down an kill that thing."

They hunted for a week up and down the mountains, all the way from Sewanee to Sherwood and beyond and never found a thing except some red and gray fox and three bobcats.

Sandy Joe and Wild West were the first ones.

It all started with their deaths.

******

She was stunningly beautiful, my mother was. When we had to go to Sewanee or Sherwood for supplies I could see it in men's eyes—I hated their eyes, even though I did not yet know that what I was seeing was lust.

When she talked or sang to me her voice and face were always gentle and loving, but they became sharp and hard when she spoke of those who were cruel. Tall and slender, there was strength in her body and smoothness in her movements; her tawny skin was tight; her long, soft, amber hair was streaked with gray. Standing beside her, I felt short, soft and stumpy. Though our differences were a terrible embarrassment to me I did not speak of it. Now I am like her, but for my mustache and shorter hair I could be her twin.

******

The night I saw her leave the house covered by what looked like the skin I climbed down the ladder and looked at her bed where she kept it. The skin was gone. I went back up to the loft and looked out the window, waiting for her return. I fell asleep.

I do not know how long I lay on the floor when I was awakened to the sound of long moaning howling. I could smell blood. In an instant I knew death was near. The sound and smell came from everywhere, from the ridges, from every side of the cabin. It filled the air above me and in me on and on until I screamed, "MAAMA MAAMA!"

The howling stopped. Only night birds called.

******

Year after year, those who were the personification of evil: child abusers, murderers of innocent people, and those who were always mean and cruel to others were either found with their throats torn out with paw prints around or on them, and there were those who disappeared. There was always a search—nothing—no animal, no human, was ever found.

My mother kept a *Farmer's Almanac* on the wall beside her bed. Dates of a full moon were circled. A day or two before those nights she became restless and paced back and forth in the yard and, now and then, she would stop and stare upward at the moon.

As the years passed I watched and listened and sniffed the air.

Slowly I began to ask questions.

Slowly I knew who she was.

Slowly she began to teach me.

******

In early Fall 1952, I left the mountains and entered Vanderbilt. I was sixteen. I had full scholarships for academics and room and board. While I knew that except for my mother I was more intelligent than anyone I had grown up with, I thought that at college and later, in medical school and later, in psychiatry I would begin to meet professors and colleagues as intelligent as I was. But there was not one.

When I left home my mother gave me the skin "for protection."

A week and a half later, the Franklin County Sheriff called to tell me my mother's body had been found by University students inside Buggytop cave. She was dead and our house was burned to the ground. I said nothing for a moment, then in a shocked voice, "O my God what"...I choked with a sob. "My mother is dead?"

"I'm fraid so son, an I'm so sorry." When he heard what sounded like sobbing he asked in a soft voice, "Son, I need to tell ya we had to go ahead an bury her cause of tha way we found her...she'd been hurt bad an had been dead for several days...I'm so sorry. Any thing I can do for ya here. When'll ya be home?"

I waited–thinking–before I answered. Then, "Sir, I...I think my mother would want me to stay here and come home during a break...I'd most likely loose my scholarships if I came home now and that would kill her she was so proud of me getting into Vanderbilt. 'Don't you dare come home. Stay there and make me proud.' That's what she would be telling you and me."

I stayed and never went back. I had all I needed from those mountains–and my mother.

******

In ten years, I finished college, medical school, Residency, had my license to practice medicine and psychiatry and eventually was hired as Assistant Professor by the Vanderbilt Department of Psychiatry and began to treat the mentally ill. More than ever, my mother would have been proud of all I had achieved.

It wasn't long before my reputation in the treatment of schizophrenia was known nationally. My writings for medical journals were highly regarded and I began to receive million dollar grants for research.

Within the next twelve years, I was elected President of the American Psychiatric Association and was the leading researcher into the genetic causes of schizophrenia and started what was to become to one of the largest investment companies in the South.

From the beginning there have been those who opposed me: stupid, jealous, narrow-minded adversaries, some powerful, some mere fleas, who threatened me, and the success of my achievements. None succeeded.

They have all disappeared in their different ways.

******

The light of the full moon streaming through the open window shines on the skin. It glistens. Following my mother's instructions I have continued to rub the salve into it every night I am here. It always feels alive and ready.

I stroke my face against the fur and whisper the words she taught me. I reach up, take the skin down, turn, open the top drawer of my desk, and take the list out.

COME SIT WITH ME

What follows tells how the title of this story originated. The events were written in my journal last year between May 22 and May 26. Now, almost a year later, I still have no satisfying explanation for what happened. My physician, who has known me for many years, believes what I experienced was a delayed reaction to loss. I am not convinced that is so.

George Spain, May 4, 2014

Wednesday, May 22, 2013. Something strange happened a few hours before sunrise this morning. I was in the den going through a stack of books piled on the footstool in front of me. The books contain letters and journals written by southern women before, during and after the Civil War. I was making notations from them for *Lucy Taggert's Six Letters,* a short story set between 1864 and 1878. I wanted to replicate, as nearly as possible, how women of that period wrote; not only what they wrote about but how they wrote it; what words they used that were unique to their time. Their letters were filled with matters of day-to-day living: God, illness, death, tidbits about their slaves whom they called "servants"; and always they were telling of their love for family and friends. Illness and death seem to be on every page—death from childbirth, battle, illness, accident and old age.

Open, on my lap was *The Children of Pride*, an exchange of hundreds of letters between members of a Georgia family during and after the war. Writing from Savannah on June 25, 1865, Mrs. Mary Jones writes to her daughter, Mrs. Mallard in Atlanta:

> *The fearful condition of our armies on the front of our own state and Virginia fills every heart with trembling. Not a day now passes but we receive the sad tidings of some friend or acquaintance slain in battle. Our country is mourning many of her sons slain in battle. Rev. Mr. Andrews and his wife were in deep sorrow for the death of a promising son killed in Virginia. Your Aunt Julia trembles for her boys now on the battlefield. Colonel Joe McCallister is said to have died bravely...Major Thompson's remains are expected out in Liberty on Monday.*

As I read of these men's deaths I thought of our third son, Adam, who was killed in Afghanistan and—in that instant—I heard a sound, so faint and indistinct it was unidentifiable. I stopped writing and listened. It seemed to have come from the wall to my left. I turned and looked upward. In the dim light of the reading lamp I saw what appeared to be a small stain coming from beneath the ceiling molding. I thought, *Oh Lord, I hope that's not water,* then, out loud I said, "Well, hell, I've got to have some coffee; it can wait a minute." And I went to the kitchen.

Before continuing with what happened this morning; I need to tell about the den and what occurred here in May 2009. The room measures fifteen by fifteen feet with a nine- foot ceiling. There are two windows: one looks out on the front yard and my wife's flower garden; the other onto a smaller garden. There is a comfortable sofa under the window. The walls are painted dark salmon; bookshelves, packed with books, line three walls; much of the furniture is quite old; valuable books and family keepsakes are on the shelves of a large oak bookcase; paintings of Indians, tiger hunts in India, and one of Jackie's great grandfather hang on the walls; in a corner, behind a brass chandelier with four globes, are two carved wooden paddles—one painted—and bows and arrows and a blow gun from the Amazon. All in all, it is an interesting room filled with family history, as is most of the house. Our entire family loves to hear, and to tell, the stories of our family's past. Every stick of furniture, every painting and every artifact brought home from our travels have been divided up already among our children and grandchildren and will go to them when I die.

Jackie died of cancer in this room in the early morning of May 25, 2009. With help from Alive Hospice we cared for her as she lay in the bed that overlooked her garden; our children oversaw the morphine that kept her from hurting. She slept most of the time. Her skin color became a yellowish pallor; there was puffing and blowing from her lips; near the end there was a rattling in her throat; her eyes were semi-open but unseeing. I saw her last breath leave her mouth as she died. We had been married almost fifty-four years. We had five children, thirteen grandchildren and **four** beautiful great grandchildren.

Three hours after her death I sent this email to family and friends:

> *This morning at 5:22, Jackie died peacefully as she took a few soft shallow breaths. The children and I were at her side gently touching her and saying, "We love you." Flowers from her garden were in small vases on the window sill beside her and the first calling of the morning birds were just on the other side of the window. How wonderful it has been having her die in her own home with her family and Sally, her loving Lab, caring for her. The room has been filled with tears, quiet laughter and love. And, oh, how we loved her! It is something how we have loved one another all these years. My*

> *heart is broken but I tell you all, "My Lord, it's been a party!"*

As I returned from the kitchen with my coffee the sound came again, this time slightly louder and longer and though still not clearly identifiable, it was rather like the deep inhaling and exhaling of someone breathing. As I stepped into the den it stopped. I set the cup down on the table beside my chair and turned on the bright chandelier lights. In the few minutes I had been out of the room the stain had grown. I got the stepstool, placed it next to the wall, stepped up and examined it. Its shape was rather like a flower petal; its deep purple color identical to the Siberian Iris–how ironic; this was Jackie's favorite color. I rubbed my fingers over the stain but felt no dampness. I sniffed my fingers; there was no scent. Whatever it was, was inside the wallboard.

I went back to the kitchen, got a ruler, came back and measured the stain: It was six inches from top to bottom, fives inches at its widest and a fourth of an inch at the bottom. I leaned forward until my nose was almost touching the wall and took in a deep breath but detected nothing.

"Well, it must be old age, like me…we're both falling apart: splotches on our flesh, bones creaking, bad plumbing and then along comes something weird."

I stepped down onto the floor, sat in my recliner, took a good sip of coffee and resumed reading letters and making notations.

Thursday, May 23, 2013 This morning, at exactly 3:30, as I was making up the bed, I heard the breathing–if that is what it was–it was louder and longer. I hurried to the den; just as I switched on the light the breathing stopped. I looked at the wall. The stain was larger. I climbed the stepstool and examined it through a magnifying glass and measured it. It had doubled in size. Magnification revealed only the deep purple; there was still no texture or odor. It measured twelve inches long by ten inches wide at its widest point and tapering to one half inch at the bottom.

Since Jackie and Adam's deaths, my daily life has become rather predictable and, except for my writing, uneventful. There is a certain comfort in this, but now it is being disturbed. I don't know why I don't simply call someone to investigate the stain. There must be a perverse curiosity in me to see if I can discover for myself what's causing these things. But then this question enters my mind: Can it be that something is happening in my brain: a slight stroke, early dementia? Or is it psychological? Has my routine, day-to-day life become so humdrum that I'm getting a peculiar enjoyment from the, as yet, unexplainable sound and stain? I remember Jackie once asking me, "Can't you ever give your mind a rest?" I don't think I gave her the right answer when I replied, "No, I can't." These strange happenings have entered my mind much like the first hint of a new story that has no direction or conclusion, only the curiosity to see where it leads. So, for the present, I'll continue my observations and measurements. As with most things that are out of the ordinary there will likely be a simple explanation. Now to bed.

Friday, May 24, 2013 It woke me again. The breathing. This time there was something more. After several breaths there was what sounded like the whisper of a word, maybe two; if they were words. I could not understand them. As before, it stopped as I entered the den. I switched on the light. The stain has doubled in size again. It is now halfway down the wall; it extends behind two pictures. Yesterday, I bought the strongest magnifying glass I could afford. I picked it up from the table. As I started to the wall, three things caught my attention: the large French print of flowers and an oil painting of cattle in a field were tilted sideways toward the sofa and there was something that brought a sharp coldness—the sofa's cushion, nearest the stain, had an impression as if someone had been sitting there; I placed a hand on the cushion; it was still warm. How could that be? No one else was in the house. I took my hand away then put it back, there was no warmth. I smoothed out the wrinkles, then stepped up on the stool and examined the stain with the magnifying glass.

My God, I could see inside the stain—it glowed and was moving. I jerked backward and almost fell; I stepped down quickly, went to the bathroom and splashed water on my face. In the mirror I could see my fear. I dried off, went back to the den and looked through the glass at the stain again; the glow and movement were gone.

Am I hallucinating? Am I going mad? Tomorrow, May the twenty-fifth, will be the fifth anniversary of Jackie's death. Is she...

Sunday, May 26, 2013 I have no explanation for why I wrote nothing yesterday. The following is all I recall –

At 5:15, I was awakened by the breathing and with it a faint voice talking. I held my breath, listening, straining to hear what was being said; the words came between the breathing, but they were spoken so softly I could not understand them. I got up and hurried into the hallway. I could see light coming from under the closed door to the den. When I had gone to bed the door had been open and the reading light turned off. I reached out to the doorknob; as I was about to grip it, I stopped and pulled my hand back.

I had dreamed of Jackie and Adam the night before. They were walking side by side down the old wagon road that winds through Lost Cove. I was following a good way behind. They stopped, turned around and motioned for me to come on. I began to run toward them and then I woke up. Though I do not believe in spirits or ghosts, I do believe that dreams may at times speak to us of our longings. I do not dream of them often but there are times, in the early morning, when I am reading in the den, that I suddenly want to see them, so I conjure them up in my mind. She is as she was those last months; I hear the shuffle of her slippers coming down the hall to the door and, as the door opens, I see her standing there smiling at me and in her soft southern voice she says, *I'm coming to sit with you, Bubbas...my Precious.* Then Adam will be standing there beside her; big and bearded, he is wiping the sleep from his eyes. And sometimes I get up and go to them with my arms out and hug them to me.

I reached out and this time gripped the knob and turned it. As the door opened, I was blinded by light; from the room came a softness of air upon my face and the fragrance of flowers and honey; within the light I heard her, *My Precious, Come sit with me.* I stepped into the room and closed the door.

www.ingramcontent.com/pod-product-compliance
Lightning Source LLC
Chambersburg PA
CBHW030427310726
48979CB00009B/1653/J

* 9 7 8 1 6 2 8 8 0 1 9 1 0 *